Brave - A Retelling of Beauty and the Beast

Kristina J Jordan

Published by Kristina J Jordan, 2021.

CHAPTER ONE

Lucie held the worn, metal bowl under her sister's chin as Marion choked and coughed. She wiped

Marion's face gently with a damp cloth as her sister collapsed in a heap. Marion closed her

eyes in exhaustion as Lucie tiptoed out the back door. She emptied the bowl into some scrub

behind the vegetable garden and rinsed it with well water. Lucie glanced up at the sky, her brow

furrowed, wondering if there was time to go to the healer, not that she could afford one these days. Shaking water off the bowl, she hurried back inside and set the bowl on the scarred kitchen table. Lucie

glanced at Marion, who was still sleeping. She wouldn't wake up for hours.

Deciding to let her sister rest, she scooped clear vegetable broth into a bowl, setting it next to

Marion's elbow. Then she splashed cold water on her face and smoothed her hair before tiptoeing

to the front stoop. Outside, Jaspar, the big cat, purred round her feet, hoping for a scratch under

the chin. Scooping the cat up into her arms, she rubbed her cheek against the soft fur, wishing she

could stay.

"Not now, Jasper, I have to work," she said.

After one last stroke, Lucie set the cat down and stepped reluctantly down the path, slowing only to

tread cautiously around muddy patches on the well-worn path to the village of Annecy. The looming

trees surrounding their cabin soon gave way to the collection of houses and shops that comprised

the village of Annecy. Between the shoemaker and the mercantile sat The Orc's Head, a squat

wooden building, the only tavern in Annecy. Lucie took a deep breath, dreading what lay inside.

Don't let her know she bothers you, Lucie reminded herself as she swung the door open.

Lucie wrinkled her nose at potent smell of fried onions as she slipped past the usual crowd' regulars

along with an assortment of travellers headed for the capital. Lucie pushed through the crowd,

heading toward the back of the tavern.

"You're late," Henri greeted her, pouring yeasty beer into large tankards.

Foam spilled over the top of one, leaving a large sticky patch on the wooden counter.

"I know, I'm sorry. Marion had a bad day; her cough's worse," Lucie said as she grabbed a cloth and

wiped up the beer puddle.

Sympathy whisked across Henri's face, quickly replaced by his usual gruff expression.

"You need to get moving. There's an extra group in today. It's about time. Goodness knows it's slow since we had the trouble with bandits...." Henri said as an uncomfortable expression crossed his

face.

"Was that them at the door?" Lucie said.

Ignoring his comment about the bandits, Lucie tied a large apron around her waist, thankful it

covered the largest patches decorating her dress.

"Those are regulars. There's group of soldiers in the annex – rough, but you can handle them. I'll

stop in time to time—keep an eye on them. Just shout if anyone bothers you," he said.

Liliana sighed. If Henri opened the back room, they would run her off her feet—it was a long way to

the kitchen from the annex. Serving the back room required extra vigilance. People were bolder

about taking liberties when they weren't being watched.

"Take these back. I'll have food ready in the minute," he said.

Henri deftly topped off the last tankard, handing the tray to Lucie.

"Took you long enough," Blanchette said when she pranced in, sniping as she tossed golden curls.

"Good luck with the soldiers."

She raised a groomed eyebrow.

"We're extra busy tonight, so don't expect help from me. Just because your father used to own half

this town doesn't mean he does now." Her voice dripped disdain.

"Sorry," Lucy said as she averted her eyes.

There was no point expecting sympathy from Blanchette. Blanchette's dislike of Lucie had intensified

over the past two years—becoming so hateful Luce dreaded going to The Orc's Head. Blanchette

glared before flouncing off, swishing her skirt with her hips.

Lucie balanced her tankards, carefully edging the door open. The annex was noisy, hot, and judging

from flushed cheeks and raucous laughter, the soldiers had been drinking for hours. She internally

cursed Henri for sending her back there alone as she dodged a hand reaching out to pat her

backside. She couldn't afford to offend—she depended on this job. Especially with Marion too ill to

take in in sewing. Lucie set the tankards down on the long table, avoiding leering eyes. If only father

would return with the lost caravans. They'd move back home and leave the cabin in the woods.

Marion would get well. Lucie pushed away fanciful thoughts as she gathered up an armful of empty

tankards for the kitchen.

Henri scooped the hot, fragrant stew into bowls and sliced steaming bread onto plates. Lucie

averted her eyes as her stomach grumbled. Her lunch, a thin bowl of soup, was hours ago. Henri was

kind about giving the barmaids dinner—after work. Sometimes he even slipped packages of food for

Lucie to take home to share with Marion.

"Mind yourself and let me know if they give you any trouble," Henri said.

He replaced the ladle in the stew pot, turning to slide the bread from the oven. Steam filled the warm kitchen with the yeasty smell of baking.

"Don't worry, Lucie knows just what to do with soldiers," Blanchette smirked as she waltzed in with a stack of empty plates. "Another tankard of cider and three bowls of stew, please? And here, Thomas sent this."

Blanchette plunked a handful of copper coins in Henri's hand. He slid them into his pocket. All coins went into the safe box at night. Only Henri and Izzie kept the key.

Lucie loaded her arms with food to take back to her tables.

"Hey there pretty girl, extra service tonight?" a hulking bearded man leered at her as she set his tankard at his elbow.

He ran a hand down his long stringy beard, a few stray crumbs knocking them onto the sticky table. Lucie took a hurried step back from the scent of unwashed hair and managed not to grimace.

She would be fine if she ignored him, Lucie convinced herself. She pretended not to hear his comment, quickly setting down another tankard of cider.

"I'm talking to you." his voice grew louder and more insistent.

Lucie gulped; this man had no intention of being ignored.

"Sorry, we only serve food and drink here," she said.

She faltered as she set down another tankard, its contents sloshing as it thumped the wooden table.

He reached for Lucie's arm, grabbing tight and jerking her toward himself.

"You sure about that?" He narrowed his eyes.

Aware she was off from the rest of the tavern, Lucie's eyes darted toward the door. Wondering if

Henri would hear her if she shouted.

"No, yes, I mean I'm sure," she stammered, flinching away from stale beery breath in her face.

"Leave the girl alone, Michel," the man next to him elbowed him in the ribs. "You'll upset the locals;

this is the only tavern in Annecy."

He let go of her arm. She skidded back, her worn slippers sliding on a puddle of beer on the stone

floor. She fell to the ground, nearly knocking over the table. Michel roared with laughter.

"Serves you right," he said. He slapped his knee with a meaty fist.

Cheeks flaming, Lucie climbed to her feet, rubbing the back of her skirt surreptitiously. That would

bruise. She gave the helpful friend a nod of thanks and turned away, embarrassed at the pity in his

eyes.

The night dragged on. Through careful manoeuvring, Lucie avoided both Michel and Blanchette

much to her relief. Finally, the soldiers stumbled back out to the cobblestone street, shouting and

pushing.

As Lucie gathered plates, her eye caught a glint of silver under an earthenware bowl. The bowl

Michel's friend had been eating from. Lucie snatched up the plate, revealing a large silver coin. She

seized it, running after the soldiers.

"Excuse me," she puffed, spotting Michel's friend whistling as he strolled toward the market square.

"You—you dropped this."

She held out the coin she had been clutching. Michel's friend winked, one side of his mouth turned up in a lazy grin.

"It's yours. A tip," he said.

Lucie stared at the coin. Tips were rare, almost unheard of, in an establishment like The Orc's Head.

Even with the steady stream of travellers trickling through to the city. But a silver? Most tips were a

copper—maybe two. She felt the weight of the coin warm her hand, speechless.

'Are you sure?' Lucie stammered awkwardly, suddenly aware of her stained apron and unpinned

hair.

He looked down at her kindly, brown eyes friendly in his tanned face. "Of course. You earned it."

"Are you coming, Peto?" a member of his party slapped him on the back.

Peto smiled again, disappearing in a rush of cold air. Dazed, Lucie slid the coin in her apron pocket

and opened the tavern door. She bumped into Blanchette, who glared, unpleasant expression

marring her pretty face.

Let her glare, Lucie thought, too overwhelmed by the kind gesture to feel the slight. She could afford one of Althea's healing tincture's now. She patted her pocket protectively.

"Won't make a difference, you still have to go home to that hovel tonight," Blanchette sniffed,

tossing her hair back. "And you're crazy if you ever think your father is coming back with those

caravans."

"Or he's wandered too close to the forest." Blanchette was joined by Liliana, who sidled up to

her—laughing at her Blanchette's joke.

Lucie shot her former best friend a pained look. Liliana lifted her head proudly and stared back

without an ounce of sympathy. The missing caravans had cost Liliana's father his business—she

never missed an opportunity to needle Lucie about it.

Blanchette and Liliana turned, pretending to be busy at the bar when Henri and Izzie, his wife,

bustled in.

"You girls must be starving." Izzie exclaimed. "Finish cleaning and we'll sit for a bite. It was a busy

night, the soldiers paid well, and the good news is they'll be here a while."

Izzie hummed in satisfaction as doled portions of stew into earthenware bowls.

"Really? How long?" Liliana quirked an eyebrow, exchanging a significant glance with Blanchette.

Lucie stayed quiet. She wasn't sure how she felt about that. The bearded man had made her pretty

uncomfortable. But—her mind wandered to the heavy silver piece hidden in her pocket. There were some kind ones among them. Maybe it wouldn't be so bad. And if the tavern stayed busy, it meant more work for her.

"King Erich wants more protection along the caravan road. They're building an outpost nearby. After what happened with the caravans before..." Izzie's voice trailed off and she slid her eyes toward Lucie.

Everyone knew the bandits were the reason Lucie and her sisters were thrust into poverty. It was a subject people studiously avoided, resorting to whispers and pitying looks. It rankled, but the alternative was the outright bitterness shown to her by those who had depended on her father's caravans.

Liliana and Lucie had been best friends until the caravans disappeared, causing Liliana's father to lose his thriving mercantile. Liliana blamed Pierre and Lucie by default for their spiralling financial ruin. Lucie turned from Liliana's bitter expression and stared at a crack in the floorboards.

"It's a good idea," she said, forcing the words out.

Much to Lucie's relief, Izzie changed the subject.

"There's plenty of stew left," she said. "I'll send some bread back for Marion. It might help her feel better—get her strength back."

Lucie's stomach rumbled again. Her meager lunch of watery soup had been too long ago.

"That sounds delicious," Lucie said.

She slid onto the long bench and picked up her spoon. Across the table, Liliana and Blanchette whispered and giggled—no doubt at her expense. The savoury stew turned to mush in Lucie's mouth.

Lucie clutched her bread tight against her chest as the long shadows slithered across the road. Don't be so silly, she chided herself as little cabin emerged through the dim light. The old door creaked as she slipped inside. The fire had fizzled out.

Lucie fumbled through the dark for kindling and flint. Soon a cozy glow filled the darkness with flickering light, and warmth seeped into the chilly air. Lucie shook her head when she saw the half empty bowl of soup by Marion's side. Picking up the cold bowl, she leaned in close to her older sister. Marion's breathing was a mere whisper, but the rattle was easing.

Lucie covered the bowl and shivered her way into her narrow loft bed—so different from the soft feather bed and down comforter from two years ago. Everything differed from two years ago. From the moment Prince Frederich's brand-new ship washed up in pieces along the coast, everything had gone downhill in Lovan.

Bandits were bolder and bolder, freely roaming the trade routes threading between Iasia and Lovan.

Pierre lost all his caravans, leaving the girls with a mountain of debt and angry townspeople. Even the forest seemed different these days – more alive...dangerous. Lucie felt it every time she walked

the narrow path into Annecy. She closed her eyes as her toes warmed under the ratty quilt.

Exhausted by the long day, she fell asleep.

CHAPTER TWO

A loud rattle startled Lucie; her eyes snapped open. The bright morning sun streamed across her

face as she rubbed her eyes and brushed back tumbling hair. Another bang, someone moving things

around in the kitchen. Lucie tiptoed to the opening in the loft and peered down into the kitchen. It

was Katherine—rummaging through a large satchel.

"Katherine? I wasn't expecting you today," Lucie grinned at her sister, skipping down the narrow

steps.

"Mary's got a big weaving job coming up, but the shipment of thread never arrived, so I changed my

day off. Look, I brought eggs and bacon," Katherine said, fishing six brown eggs from her bulging

satchel and setting them gently in a wooden bowl.

"How's Marion?" she cast a sidelong glance toward the bed in the corner. Still sleeping, Marion lay

curled under the quilt in the same position Lucie had left her the night before.

Lucie lowered her voice, whispering: "She's been asleep since yesterday afternoon. I'm worried

about the cough though. It was so harsh yesterday she vomited. I'm going to Althea's later; she'll make her a remedy."

"The herbalist? Won't that be expensive?" Worry etched Katherine's face.

"I have extra money. I got a tip last night." Lucie held up the silver coin proudly. "Henri said I could

keep it."

"But shouldn't we save for winter? What happens when snow falls and the roads close? If business is

bad, Henri won't keep you at Orc's Head."

"I know Kat," Lucie met her sister's searching eyes, "but we have to help Marion. I'll have money left

over. You know Althea has a soft spot for us. She'll not charge much—if anything."

Lucie splashed water on her face and dried it with a rough cloth, hanging it carefully on a peg when

she finished.

"While you're at Althea's, I'll weed the garden. I've hunched over Izzie's new curtains all week."

Katarina stretched her arms over her head and rubbed the back of her neck. "It was the big loom,

too. It leaves me so stiff."

"The rhubarb is ripe. You can take some to Mary," Lucie said. She sliced off a piece of bread and took

the mug of black tea Katherine offered.

After breakfast, Lucie strolled through the warm sunshine, heading toward Annecy. Plucking the last

summer wildflowers along the way, she tucked them into her braided hair. There wasn't time or

inclination to plant flowers in the garden this year, and Lucie missed them. Lucie wistfully remembered their old gardens. The entire village commented on the size of Marion's roses, but

Lucie's favourite spot had been a small seat near the fountain. Lucie spent many a happy hour

loafing there, the pleasant tinkling a backdrop to the adventure book she read in secret past

Marion's watchful eye.

Although Lucie brought a few rose cuttings with her to the cabin; the damp and dark of the forest

quickly stifled them. Within months, they withered and died. She decided she would get seeds or

cuttings and plant next year. Izzie grew roses grown behind the kitchen garden of The Orc's

Head—not elegant like Marion's, but hardier, more suited to the forest climate. Cheered by this

thought, and looking forward to visiting Althea, Lucie tripped up the stone path to the healer's

cottage. Nestled at the edge of the village, Althea's cottage was half hidden in a vast herb garden.

Althea preferred to grow her own, insisting they increased the potency of her remedies and

tinctures.

"Althea?" Lucie knocked before peeping in the half-opened door.

"Hello dear," Althea said as she hobbled across the colourful braided rug.

Althea's cottage was cosy; bunches of dried herbs hung from the kitchen rafters, and jars and bottles

lined the shelves. Cinnamon and cloves mixed with the more homely scent of sweet rosemary and thyme to perfume the air. A town the size of Annecy was lucky to have a healer of Althea's calibre.

Even caravaners and travellers sought Althea out when passing through. In turn, they provided her with herbs, spices, and other mysterious ingredients from far-flung locations. Rumour had it, even King Erich's doctor occasionally sent the castle healer for Althea's remedies. Who knew if there was truth in that rumour though. Althea wasn't one to share secrets.

"Come, sit," Althea urged Lucie to the rocking chair at the fireplace. "I never see you anymore. How are you and your sisters?"

"That's why I'm here." Lucie cupped the mug of tea Althea pressed on her. A plate of sticky buns followed, still warm from the bakery.

"What's wrong, dear?" Worry flashed across Althea's face. She nudged a sleeping cat from the other chair and sat.

'Not me, Marian. It's been ages, and she isn't over the cough," Lucie explained.

"What kind of cough? Chesty?" Immediately. Althea hobbled to her wooden mixing table. Lucie followed, perching on a three-legged stool. Lucie loved watching Althea at her work.

"I know what she needs." Althea picked through her herbs, choosing a spring of something brown and withered that somehow filled the air with a fresh, clean scent.

She crushed it with a grey lumpy substance spooned from a jar, before adding a drop of murky liquid
that made it all bubble and fizz.

"This will help her eat better." Althea smiled to herself in satisfaction and added another drop of the
liquid.

"Two pinches in hot tea three times a day." Althea added a dried root before scooping the mixture
into a small paper packet, folding it tightly and securing it with a drop of wax.

"That's it?" Lucie looked dubiously at the small packet that Althea pressed into her hand.

"Yes," Althea's faded eyes crinkled.

"Um, what should I pay you? Is this enough?" Lucie held out the silver coin.

"Well, I hate to take anything from you, Lucie. You know how I feel about you and your sisters. But I
suppose you won't be happy unless I do." Althea pushed Lucie's hand away.

Lucie shook her head, firm. "Althea, you've done so much already."

"Fine." Althea reluctantly reached into a leather bag around her neck, fishing out some smaller silver
coins. She handed them to Lucie in exchange for the larger one.

"You and your sisters stay safe. If Marion grows more of those magnificent roses, bring me some
rose hips. They were wonderful in my winter fever restorative. And don't worry about your father.

He'll be home soon." Althea smiled kindly, knowing eyes following as Lucie picked her way down the
garden path.

Lucie was so distracted avoiding the mud that she completely missed Liliana, bumping headfirst into
her former friend.

"Sorry," Lucie said. She took a hasty step back, rubbing her forehead.

"Watch where you're going," Liliana snapped. "You're so clumsy. Oh, unless you are making eyes at
soldiers." She raised her eyebrows, giving Lucie a challenging look.

"What?" Lucie's mouth gaped; she took another hasty step back.

"You heard me. Blanchette saw you flirting with those... those thugs last night. Did you think he
might actually like you? They felt sorry for you – like everyone else does." Bitterness poured from
Liliana's voice, forcing Lucie back another step.

Lucie's eyes stung; her throat was tight. She stiffened her spine, squashing the instinct to run.

"Pardon?"

"I, for one, don't feel sorry for you. Pierre ruined us. You deserve everything you get," Liliana said.

Huffing, she flicked her hair and stomped up the path, swinging last year's skirts behind her.

Lucie turned, running after her. Maybe without Blanchette whispering in her ear, Liliana would see it
wasn't her fault, Lucie thought.

"Liliana, you know bandits overrun the forest—and the trade routes. Father — Pierre — is doing

everything he can to get the caravan back. Please..."

Liliana's only answer was to turn and glare at Lucie and march on.

Lucie blinked back the tears glazing her eyes, refusing to let them fall. Especially not in front of

Liliana, who had overnight gone from being her best friend to barely being able to tolerate her

presence. She sighed, heading back into the gloom of the forest.

CHAPTER THREE

Lucie carefully unwound the twine that held the packet of herbs, tipping Althea's herb mixture into a
mug of tea.

"Marian, drink this. It's from Althea." The heady, sweet scent of the herbs Althea used tickled Lucie's
nostrils as she brought the cup to Marion.

Marion opened weary eyes, struggling to sit.

"Althea sent this tincture you," Liliana repeated. She held the gently steaming cup to Marion's dry
lips. The scent wafted toward her, filled the entire room with its sweetness. Marion sipped at the
hot liquid, colour returning to pale cheeks as she swallowed.

"You'll feel better in no time." Forced cheerfulness is her voice, Lucie held the cup for Marion to take
another drink.

"Back so soon?" Katherine said, carrying a basketful of vegetables. "Look, our beets are huge." She
held up a fist sized root, sending a shower of dirt crumbling to the wooden floorboards. "Mary's
vegetables don't grow nearly as big as ours do."

"That's wonderful." Lucie pasted on a smile, averting her eyes from the dirt covering the floor. "Will

19

we make a stew for dinner? Were there any onions?"

Katherine poked through the basket.

"Just these smallish ones. And You never told me about the apple tree behind the shed. I didn't

know there were fruit trees so deep in the woods. If we gather more, we can sell fruit at market day

in the fall or sell them to the bakery." The practical Katherine's face lit up with the possibilities.

Lucie hesitated. "The woods make me nervous; I haven't looked for apples. There's been—noises."

"Noises? What noises? Like the wind? Lucie, we don't believe all those superstitions. There's no

magic in Lovan. You're listening to too many of Althea's stories."

Lucie shot Katherine a stubborn look, crossing her arms. "I heard something."

"Don't be silly, that's an old wives' tales. There's nothing fiercer than deer or foxes in those woods,"

Katherine insisted, sitting at the table she stroked Jasper, who had been lurking at her ankles asking

for attention. Her voice faltered, not as convincing as it could be.

Marion finished her tea, her eyes brighter, she joined the conversation. "I heard noises too," she

said.

"You did?" Lucie and Katherine stared at Marion.

"Yes, howling – like a wolf. While you were working at The Orc's Head last night. I was going to tell

you when you got home, but I fell asleep."

"Are you sure you weren't dreaming?" Lucie asked.

She cringed, thinking of her long walks home, only moon-light between her and forest.

"There hasn't been a wolf spotted in forever.... generations. Even Althea's never seen one in this

country, the wolves always stop at the Iasian border."

"I wasn't dreaming," Marion said.

A troubled expression flashed through Marion's eyes. "I worry about you at The Orc's Head late at

night. Are you sure Henri and Izzie don't have a spare room? You could share with Blanchette," she

suggested.

Lucie grimaced as she took the empty cup from Marion and washed it. "I suppose I could ask. But

you know Blanchette despises me, especially since last night."

"Why, what happened last night?" Marion's eyes snapped to Lucie's face.

Lucie explained how Peto gave her the silver coin. "I'm al-most positive Blanchette saw him give me

the coin. She was standing with her nose at the window when I came in the door. You know she

hates it when anyone else gets attention."

Marion leaned against the lumpy pillow.

"Blanchette has always been snippy with you, but she's jeal-ous. You just have to stop running away;

it never works. But when I get well, I'll take in sewing—at least you won't have to see her every night

then," Marion said.

"I don't always run away from things," Lucie argued, cut-ting the tops off the beets, trying not to stain her hands with the red juice. "Anyway, maybe you won't have to take in sewing. Father will

come back, maybe with good news. Maybe he'll find the caravans."

"I'd love a new dress," Katherine rubbed ruefully at a large smudge of dirt on what used to be her

best dress. "No boy will look at me wearing this old rag."

"Wouldn't some curtains and a rug be nice?" Marion covered her knees with the thin blanket.

"Something to make it more cozy around here."

Lucie sliced off the last beet top, wiping her stained hands on a rag. "New things would be nice, they

really would; but all I really need is everyone together again. Together, safe and healthy. It's been

months since Father went to look for the caravans. Long enough to make the trip twice."

"Do you think Blackie got hurt or sick?" Katherine said. She sorted through the basket, pulling out a

handful of carrots.

"No. Blackie's an old horse, but strong and healthy. Father's probably just chasing down a lead,"

Lucie said, taking out their broom. She began to sweep the floor.

That night the Orc's Head was busier than usual.

"You're in the annex again," Henri said in a terse voice, handing her the tankards he was busy pouring.

Lucie was carrying them carefully in when a stray bit of gossip stopped her in her tracks.

"Prints the size of your head," Lucie overheard one man mutter to his neighbor, gesturing.

Lucie slowed, hovering as she served the tankards. She eyed the speaker closely. It was one of the

soldiers from last night. He took the tankard, tossing it back with a frown. The mood was different

tonight, quieter. Instead of the boisterous hubbub, the group was uneasy. Nervous.

"Whatever they're paying us isn't enough," she heard another soldier complain as she served the

remaining drinks. Lucie strained her ears, hoping for more information.

"I thought it was supposedly safe near the capital. I mean, this is Lovan. But whatever left those

footprints isn't natural, and I've been to Iasia... I've seen things. And the howling?" the man shook

his head, staring glumly into his beer.

Hands empty, Lucie headed to the kitchen, passing Blanchette.

"Father says you're sleeping with me tonight," Blanchette snipped unhappily.

"What? Why?"" Lucie's eyes rounded in dismay before she politely attempted to hide her distress.

"Not that I mind ... but Marion will expect me. She'll worry."

"Oh, don't pretend; I know you don't want to stay any more than I want you here. It's because of

that creature." Blanchette narrowed her eyes and gave Lucie a look of disgust.

"Creature?" Lucie pasted on an innocent expression, hoping Blanchette would take the bait.

"They're all talking about it. The soldiers working on the outpost saw prints, and apparently they're gigantic." Blanchette leaned close, whispering, so intent on sharing juicy gossip she temporarily forgot her hatred for Lucie. "They think it's a wolf or a bear. But I don't know ... it would have to be a tremendous bear to make prints that gigantic. Unless ..."

"Unless?" Lucie breathlessly waited for Blanchette to continue.

"Unless it's a magical creature." Blanchette widened her eyes, milking every possible bit of drama out of the story.

Lucie scoffed. "Magical creatures don't exist. Not in Lovan."

"Well, what else could it be?" Blanchette huffed.

"You know soldiers, they're often exaggerating. Maybe it's just a really big fox or something." Lucie's words trailed off uneasily.

"Some of them heard howling. Said it positively made their blood curdle right in their veins—you know you'll have to be extra careful in that little cabin of yours, it's so close to the forest." Blanchette smirked, fidgeting coyly with the pink ribbon tying back her curls. "Wait and see, it's not just bandits we have to worry about anymore." Blanchette grinned when Lucie's face paled.

"You know there's no magic in Lovan, you've been listening to too many Iasian stories." Lucie pressed her lips together, turning back to the kitchen.

"Did Blanchette find you?" Izzie asked, lifting the pot lid and pinching salt into the stew. The

rich, savoury steam rose from the stew, surrounding Izzie in a thick cloud.

"Yes, she told me about the footprint. Don't worry, Izzie, they're surely exaggerating. I don't want to

leave Marion on her own." Lucie ladled strew into bowls, careful not to drip thick gravy over the

edge of the pot.

Henri placed a gentle hand on Lucie's shoulder.

"I understand you girls don't get along, but don't let that put you into danger. You can go home to

Marion in the morning. She'll be fine if locks the door tight. How is she today anyway? Any better?"

He steered the conversation away from the sleeping arrangements.

Lucie's face brightened.

"Yes, I got a remedy from Althea; I think it's working. She ate her entire dinner and even took extra

bread. She loved your bread, Izzie," Lucie said.

Izzie beamed as she began peeling more potatoes, her knife glinting as it flew through the air.

"That's wonderful. You girls have had a pack of trouble and didn't deserve a lick of it. I wouldn't wish

ill of you. Now, go serve the stew before it's cold; we'll settle the sleeping arrangements later."

Henri gave Lucie another pat on the back as she left with the heavy tray.

As she wove through the crowded room, Lucie felt a prickle of awareness in the back of her neck.

She turned to see steady brown eyes fixed on her. Peto.

"It seems we meet again," he said. His smile was warm his rugged face.

"Thanks for the tip last night," she said.

Lucie smiled shyly, setting the steaming bowl in front of him, adding a plate of freshly sliced bread

topped with a golden lump of butter. "You didn't have to give me that coin. It was far too

generous."

"It was nothing—if those soldiers give you trouble, just let me know. I'm Captain Peto. My soldiers

are kind souls, but one or two are rough around the edges." He slashed a pointed look at Michel,

who had behaved today, not even sparing Lucie a second glance.

"Thanks," she said. Lucie shifted her feet and clutched the empty tray against her chest.

Lucie felt Blanchette's gaze stabbing her as she returned to the kitchen. Wonderful, Blanchette has

noticed Captain Peto and wants his attention. No wonder she was extra snippy last night. Lucie

hadn't realized he was a captain – a fact Blanchette would have ferreted out immediately. No

wonder she was jealous.

Finally, The Orc's Head quieted. Captain Peto hung back, waiting as the last few soldiers trickled

out.

"This is for you." He pressed another large silver piece into Lucie's palm. Astonished, Lucie pushed

it back.

"It's too much," she insisted, lowering her lashes.

Rodrick's eyes twinkled down at her. "I insist." He closed her fingers around the silver and hurried

to catch up with his men.

"What did he give you? Another coin?" Lucie turned to Blanchette, peering nosily over her

shoulder. "Did the Captain give you silver?" Her eyes glittered.

Lucie drew back, clutching her hand protectively around the coin.

"Yes, but I didn't ask for it. Henri told me to take it."

Blanchette huffed, "That should be mine. I saw him first."

"Girls, come for dinner," Izzie beckoned from the warmth of the kitchen.

Blanchette and Lucie sat on the wooden bench and ate their dinner. It surprised Lucie to find that

Blanchette was pleasant, even taking dirty plates and offering to help wash up when she finished.

Lucie stretched and yawned as she put the last spoon neatly in its slot. The kitchen shone, but her

back ached from the long afternoon in the garden and her feet were sore from running back and

forth to the annex.

"Ready for bed?" Blanchette smiled, showing milky white teeth. "I've made the spare trundle.

Liliana's brother took her home tonight. You can have it. Come on, I'll get you my old nightgown."

Lucie followed Blanchette up the narrow staircase, quickly changing into the clean linen nightgown

Blanchette offered her; leaving her apron and dress folded next to the bed. She yawned again,

pressing cold toes against the warm brick Blanchette placed at the bottom of the bed, and pulled the

soft, sweet smelling quilt to her nose.

"I'll be back in a minute, I forgot to lock the pantry," Blanchette said.

Leaving Lucie in darkness, Blanchette whisked the candle away, disappearing down the stairs. Lucie

had every intention of staying awake until she returned. But the soft pillow soon claimed her, and

she fell asleep.

CHAPTER FOUR

Raised, angry voices dragged Lucie from the depths of a heavy sleep. She struggled out of the warm quilt, yawning and blinking grit from her tired eyes.

"What's the commotion about?" Lucie asked Blanchette, stirring in the other bed.

"Stay here, I'll go find Father," Blanchette replied. She then shrugged on a dress and scampered away, leaving Lucie alone in her bedroom. As Lucie fastened the last button, heavy footsteps pounded up the wooden staircase.

"What's wrong?" Lucie said, her eyes rounded as Henri barged through the door. His usually pleasant expression was cold and stern. Blanchette slipped in after him – a sly, triumphant expression slid across her face.

"Lucie sneaked downstairs. I heard her creeping around," Blanchette's voice whined, high and plaintive. "She must have thought I was asleep."

"I didn't go downstairs last night," Lucie protested, icy fingers of dread creeping up her spine. Her eyes darted to Blanchette. What was she planning? Blanchette's blue eyes gleamed with satisfaction, a sly smile curling the edges of her mouth.

29

"Don't lie. Check her apron, Daddy, I watched her put something there," Blanchette pouted, pointing

at Lucie's apron folded neatly beside the bed.

"You mean the silver coin? Peto gave that to me; I showed the coin to Izzie last night." Lucie bit her

lip.

"Coin? We're not talking about your measily coin," Blanchette's voice rang, triumphant. "We're talking about

the money from the safe box. Someone stole the coin last night."

"I didn't steal your silver from the safe box. I don't even know where the safe box is," Lucie

protested feebly. A feeling of dread pierced her chest.

"If you didn't take our money, it won't be in your apron. Should we search?" Eyes hard, Blanchette

grabbed Lucie's apron. Lucie blanched, knowing even before Blanchette lifted the apron it would be

heavy with stolen silver.

"It wasn't me..." Lucie's voice weakened as gleaming silver coins spilled through Henri's fingers,

shimmering like water against his rough skin.

"Lucie, how could you? We stood by you when Pierre's caravans disappeared, gave you a job, kept

food on your table." Henri's disappointed voice caused hot tears to prick the back of Lucie's eyes.

Her throat swelled as a coin slipped from Henri's hand, rolling under the bed. Blanchette quickly

scrambled after it.

"I suppose it makes sense. You're just a thief and cheat like your father." Blanchette dramatically handed the coin to Henri and dusted her hands, propping them on her hips.

"Blanchette," Henri protested unconvincingly. "Be sensible. There might be another explanation."

He slid his eyes away from Lucie, discomfort etched across his face.

"Sensible? Sensible?" Blanchette screeched, her voice quivering. "Clearly, she's a thief! She can't

work here now. What's she going to steal next? The horses? The chickens? We'll be left with

nothing. You have to lock her up."

Lucie shot Henri a beseeching look, twisting her hands in her lap. Surely he could see Blanchette

engineered this. Betrayed her.

"No, we'll not lock her up," Henri relented. "But, Lucie, you can't work here. Ever."

Blanchette tossed Lucie a smug grin, quickly replaced by a frown as Henri turned sternly to his

daughter. "Blanchette, not a word to anyone. It wouldn't be fair to Katherine and Marion.

Understood?"

"Yes Daddy," Blanchette cooed, folding her hands demurely.

"Leave when you're ready," Henry told Lucie. He unsmilingly took the silver, still wrapped in the

apron. Blanchette followed, tossing a smirk over her shoulder before she slammed the door.

CHAPTER FIVE

Betrayed. Alone. Vilified.

Lucie huddled into her worn cloak, slipping out the tavern door into bright sunlight. Fighting

threatening tears until Annecy disappeared behind thick trees, she dragged a shaking hand over her

face. How would she face Marion and Katherine?

She'd planted enough food in the garden for summer, maybe fall, but winter? Lucie shuddered.

Katherine would be all right. Katherine's weaving job at Mary's would sustain her as long as plenty of

orders came in — if Blanchette kept her mouth shut. Knowing Blanchette, that was an unlikely

scenario. Lucie kicked a clod of dirt, whimpering when her bruised toe protested against the rough

treatment.

Lucie slowed, hesitating at the ramshackle cabin door, hand hovering above the latch. Inside she

heard a familiar rumbling voice. With a low cry, she flung the door open, flying into Pierre's

outstretched arms.

"You're home! You're home! You're home!" she said. She wept into his tobacco-scented coat as he swung her around the tiny room, knocking over a wooden chair.

"You two!" Marion exclaimed, laughing. She sat with a blanket over her knees, cheeks rosy with happiness.

"When did you get home? Did you find the caravans?" Brimming with questions, Lucie plopped into the nearest seat.

Pierre returned to his chair, shaking his head. "Nothing. I travelled up and down the entire caravan route and nothing. Not a scrap of cloth nor a wisp of hair. It's like they never existed. Ghosts.

According to my sources, they made it through Florin and past Havre."

"Havre?" Marian questioned. "They travelled past the Iaisan border?" The sisters exchanged glances.

In Iasia, magic could explain the disappearance — but in Lovan? Impossible.

"Could we still find the caravans? Is there any chance?" Lucie asked. "Perhaps the caravan master left the path for the forest. Maybe the bandits forced them to hide?"

Pierre scratched his chin. "They've been missing too long. Whatever's happened to the caravans, we're going to have to give them up for lost."

"But the families. They've been working your caravan route for years. What possibly could have happened?"

Pierre's expression tightened, his eyes hard. "Magic."

"Here in Lovan? That's not possible," Lucie said as she hovered on the edge of her seat.

"I wouldn't believe magic existed in Lovan if I didn't see it with my own eyes." Pierre leaned back in

the rickety chair, threading his hands together.

"I was a few hours ride from Havre. A vendor spotted the caravans at Market Square, so I was extra

vigilant for any sign of them. Blackie and I reached the giant oak forest, the king's forest. The ride

exhausted Blackie, she's not young anymore. So, I searched for a safe place to camp, somewhere

secure from bandits. We left the path, but the oak trees grew thick. We wandered and got lost. I

eventually let Blackie have her head. She's sensible and knows to find her way home. I knew we'd

find our way when the sun rose. That's when I came upon a giant chateau, nearly a castle."

"A chateau in King Erich's forest? No one's even allowed to hunt there. Was it a hunting lodge?"

Lucie gripped her hands together, mesmerised by her father's story.

Pierre shook his head. "It wasn't King Erich's lodge. That's beside the road, clearly marked. This

chateau is a complete mystery. I've memorized that route like the back of my hand. It's unthinkable I

wouldn't know of a chateau of that magnitude on the caravan route."

"Did you go in?" Lucie held her breath, eyes glued to her father's face.

"I did. The gate was only latched, not locked. I was hoping to find shelter for Blackie to rest overnight.

I went in the gate, knocked at the front entrance. No one answered. I thought I'd check around the

side courtyard, the kitchen entrance. I didn't see anyone; the place was completely deserted. But

then..." Pierre paused significantly. The two sisters leaned forward in anticipation.

"I heard... a voice. Quite close — but invisible."

"A voice? A ghost?" Lucie interrupted; her blue eyes suspicious.

"A human voice. But when I searched the courtyard, I saw no one. I heard the invisible voice again at

my elbow. It was as close together as we are." Pierre gestured with his hand, waving at the three

feet of space between himself and Lucie.

"She was friendly, and I'm no stranger to magic. I stayed. Besides, I was curious; I reasoned the voice

didn't want to harm me. When the voice invited me to eat dinner, I did. I followed her into a huge

dining room, alone. Food filled the table. One plate, one glass, one setting, like they knew I was

staying. Delicious food. I don't know when I've last had anything that fine. The tenderest roast beef

I've ever had, a beautiful wine, dessert, cheese, chocolates, everything."

"What about Blackie?" Marion asked, tugging the blanket tight around her knees.

"When I finished eating, a lamp arrived. It was floating as if someone was holding it. The invisible voice spoke again, bidding me follow, so I did. The lamp bobbed through the chateau, across a

courtyard, to a stable – a lovely stable, with a fresh straw bed for Blackie. There were oats, hay and

water and Blackie ate like a king. It was the strangest experience, a brush moving through the air,

grooming Blackie, rubbing him until he shone like glass."

"What did Blackie think? Was he spooked?" Lucie imagined the floating brush in her mind's eye. It all

seemed too fantastical to be real.

Pierre shook his head. "Blackie was just glad to have shelter from the cold. When Blackie saw the oats

and hay, he was very pleased. I'm surprised he didn't get indigestion."

"After I saw to Blackie, the invisible voice led me to a bedroom. It was a massive, beautiful

stateroom. I couldn't believe they meant it for me. Velvet drapes, with a big carved bed and gold

everywhere. I mean, this was the most magnificent room I've ever seen. Everything there was

strangely old-fashioned, preserved for centuries. Intricate tapestries, rich carpets, damask bedding."

Pierre's eyes held a faraway look.

"Katherine would love that," Lucie said. Fabrics and textiles held a peculiar fascination for their

weaving sister.

"She would. I wish Katherine could have seen it." Pierre smiled. "I slept, and when I woke in the

morning, everything sat ready. My boots were cleaned and polished, my clothes washed and

pressed, breakfast was spread out. In the stable, they watered and fed Blackie. I've never seen him so

shined up in my life, and they cleaned his tack until I could
see my face reflected."

"Did you learn who owns the chateau?" Pierre's haunting
story captivated Lucie.

Pierre paused and a shadow crossed his face. "On the way
home, a long lane led to an enormous

iron gate, with a rose garden surrounding it. I wanted to
bring you girls one rose. I thought surely

they wouldn't miss it after everything else I received. There
were hundreds of big, beautiful roses of

every colour, sweet-scented roses. You girls would have
loved them. I reached out and picked one as

I rode by, thinking I would slip it in the saddlebag. And
that's when I saw him."

"Saw who?" Lucie bit her lip in anticipation. Her father's
face turned grim, eyes tightening.

"A giant beast. I don't know what else I could call that
monstrous creature. It stood on two legs, like

us, but it was huge – at least eight feet tall. And it could
talk. In fact, it sounded human. I've seen my

share of magic, but this was different."

"What did the beast say?" Lucie searched her father's eyes.
She knew by his terrible expression that

the next part of this story would not be pleasant.

"The beast was furious, livid. It said, 'How dare you steal
from the king's garden after all my

hospitality?' I apologized profusely. I told him I was sorry,
I just wanted the rose for my daughters, I

had nothing else to bring them. He told me I would have to pay the price for stealing." Pierre

stopped; a devastated expression flashing through his eyes.

"What was the beast's price?" Lucie asked, twisting the end of her hair anxiously.

"My crime was on royal land, the king's land. The beast demanded I go back and perform a term of

service, the penalty for stealing from the king."

Marion frowned. "Surely, he can't enforce the penalty. The royal family outlaws magic in Lovan.

They have banned it for hundreds of years. He shouldn't even be in the king's forest. The beast is

probably breaking the law himself."

Horror washed through Lucie's veins, she stood, pacing the floor. "That law is archaic, everyone

knows King Erich would never enforce it, that creature can't possibly think you're going to work for

him in some haunted castle, chateau, whatever it is ... How long is this term of service?"

Pierre's eyes filled with sadness. "The beast offered to let me send one of you girls instead. I would

die before I let that creature take one of you."

"Can't you stay?" Lucie questioned. "The Beast would never follow you to Annecy."

Pierre bowed his head. "The beast knows where I live. If I don't return, they'll be consequences. The

creature implied as much. If magic has entered Lovan, the beast could be capable of tremendous

harm. I must go."

"I'll go!" The words burst out of Lucie's mouth before her thoughts caught up with her mouth. "Why shouldn't I? I can't go back to the Orc's Head."

Eyes narrowed, Marion swung her head toward Lucie. "Why can't you go to The Orc's Head? Did you argue with Blanchette?" Lucie gulped and Marion's face softened as she noted her distress.

"What's wrong, darling?" Marion asked. She smoothed Lucie's hair with a gentle hand. At this slight gesture of kindness, Lucie was undone. The entire story spilled out; bitter tears springing to Lucie's eyes as she remembered the injustice of it all.

"Oh, sweet girl. That's terrible. Blanchette's always been dreadful. We'll work something out. Henri will come to his senses. I know he dotes on Blanchette, but deep down he knows what she's capable of," Marion consoled Lucie.

"But your medicine. How will I pay for another dose from Althea?" Lucie sniffed, wiping her eyes.

"I'm feeling much better already." Marion stroked her soothing hand along Lucie's hair. "I'm sure once I'm over this cough, I won't need the tincture anymore. Another week and I'll be keeping up with you. If Henri doesn't come to his senses, Izzie can talk to him. She's not oblivious to Blanchette's tricks." She tweaked the end of Lucie's braid.

"But Marion, you know Blanchette will spread tales all over Annecy. I've nothing left in this village without that job. I can ride to the Château tomorrow — take the beast's service — Father can find work in the village. He'll find new merchants, build back his caravan trade again." Lucie shot Pierre a

hopeful look.

"No!" Pierre's voice rang out firmly. "No daughter of mine will suffer at that beast's mercy. The

misunderstanding with Blanchette will blow over. I've known Henri for many years. He's a good man,

he'll see the truth and rein Blanchette in. She's spoiled, but she's gone too far. I'll speak to him

myself if I must." He pressed his lips into a thin line, his eyes glittering with determination.

"But Father," Lucie protested. "If I take the term of service, I'll come back. I mean, it might be a

while, but surely, the beast allows visits. We'd be together again, eventually. And you won't have to

feed me while I sit here twiddling my thumbs."

"No, and that's final," he said. Pierre's voice was gentler, but the girls knew he meant business.

"Now, let me rest and enjoy these last two days with my girls. I'll go visit Katherine this afternoon

and tell her the news. If I send Blackie back after I get to the Chateau, you can sell her. That money

should be enough to feed you girls through this winter. While I'm there, I'll speak to Mary about

taking another weaver on. With the trade routes the way they are, she's surely going to have more

orders coming in. After all, we're not importing wool from Iasia anymore; demand will be high this

winter. I've raised three strong capable girls and you're going to be just fine. Now, Lucie, enough talk about taking the term of service. Put the kettle over the fire and boil a pot of tea."

Outwardly obedient, Lucie filled the kettle and put it over the fire, setting out the cups and leaves for

tea. But inside her mind was racing, forming a plan. She wouldn't let father go back into that forest.

Not if she had anything to do with it.

CHAPTER SIX

Floorboards creaked beneath Lucie's feet as she crept down narrow wooden steps. Pierre's gentle
snore drifted from below, covering the sound of soft footsteps as Lucie tiptoed out of the dark cabin,
into the velvety night. Clear skies left enough light for her to muddle through the tack and saddle
Blackie.

"You're going to help me find this chateau, old girl," she whispered as Blackie pressed her inquisitive
nose against her cloak. She led Blackie down the forest path, only mounting when safely out of
earshot of the cabin.

With a sense of relief, Lucie left Annecy, traveling northbound through the forest track toward
Havre. After several hours of riding, the gentle sway and the clip-clop of Blackie's hooves lulled Lucie
into nodding off. She only startled into wakefulness when Blackie flinched, half rearing. Lucie
clutched his mane, fighting to stay seated.

"What happened, old girl?" Lucie patted Blackie's neck soothingly, scanning the forest for anything
unusual.

Dappled sunlight filtered through soaring oak trees, creating shifting patterns on the forest floor.

Legends said the ancient site of the Lavonian capital lay in King's Forest, when Lovan was a magic

kingdom. Lucie had to admit, she felt a strange sort of tingling here. A buzzing sensation crawled

across her skin, leaving trails of goosebumps in its wake.

Lucie wished she had asked her father more questions about the exact location of the mysterious

chateau. Her eyes searched the forest as Blackie ambled on. Lucie had traveled well past the halfway

point to Havre and saw no sign of anything strange or unusual showing the location of the strange

chateau. If not for her father's sensible, practical nature, she would have given up, chalking it up to a

bad dream or an overactive imagination.

"Where are you, strange beast?" Lucie muttered, examining the silent trees for a path or clearing

leading to the chateau.

"Hello? I'm here to serve you," Lucie called, glad no human ears could hear her talking to the trees.

Then something caught her eye. A shimmer gleaming through the deep green foliage.

Lucie swung off Blackie, taking a few hesitant steps. Yes, there was a strange light shining in the

underbrush.

Leading Blackie off the forest path, she called in a faltering voice. "Is anyone there?" The sound

disappeared, fading into the rustling leaves.

Another burst of sparkling light. This one hovered right in front of her.

"Am I supposed to follow you?" Lucie faltered.

Another flash.

"Strange." Lucie muttered, pushing through the forest after the bobbing light. There was no path,

and a few times Lucie nearly lost sight of her strange guide as she forced her way through brambles

and underbrush and forged alternative routes around fallen trees.

"Are we almost there?" They had stopped at a small brook. Thirsty, Blackie buried his nose in the

cool, clear water. Streaks of mud covered the hem of Lucie's dress and wisps of hair escaped,

sticking to her forehead and the back of her neck.

There was no response except another brief, impatient flicker of brightness.

"All right, let's go." Lucie brushed the debris off her skirt, plunging on.

After hours that felt like days, the immense trees thinned, giving way to an ancient boulevard. Lucie

let out a sharp breath, craning her neck to gaze at a monumental structure, vast even for a chateau.

Massive iron gates, the ones Pierre had described, slowly creaked open to continue the long

boulevard. The boulevard ended at a fountain tinkling merrily in front of the imposing front

entrance.

"What is this place?" Lucie breathed in awe.

"Chateau de Chine." A musical voice at her elbow startled Lucie out from her reverie. She spun
around to find her twinkling companion had disappeared.

"You talk?" she said.

"Only at the chateau," the invisible voice answered. "The magic isn't powerful enough to use my
voice outside the gardens."

"Where are you? Why can't I see you anymore?" Lucie swung in a circle, searching for the sparkling
light.

The musical voice laughed. "That wasn't me, it was mica dust. I used it so you could see where I was
going."

"Mica dust?"

"From the quarry in the western forest," the pleasant voice answered. "Anyway, I must introduce
myself. I'm Fleur. And you must be Pierre's daughter? It's been so long since we've had human
guests here; and now two — just this week. You can't imagine how delighted we are."

"I'm Lucie. And this is Blackie." Lucie patted the horse's nose affectionately as he snuffled shifting his
feet next to her.

"You've had a long journey. Are you tired? Come on, up these stairs, I'll take you inside."

Lucie followed Fleur's voice up the grand steps leading to the large, forbidding entrance. The old-
fashioned door groaned as it opened, revealing a grand, gloomy entrance hall.

A strange chill ran down her spine as cool, musty air brushed her face. She assumed it must be

magic.

"How did the chateau get here?" she whispered in awe as they entered. A frescoed ceiling soared

above her head, and a finely made statue gleamed from a nearby alcove.

"Follow me." Fleur ignored her question, her voice brisk.

"How will I see the direction you're going?" Lucie turned her head, hoping for some sign of Fleur,

then winced when she saw the marks her muddy slippers left across the shining marble floor.

"Oh, silly me! I forgot, wait here a minute." She left Lucie peering around the echoing hall. Presently

a bobbing candle appeared. "I forgot people can't see me. Just follow the candle." Fleur instructed.

Lucie obediently followed the floating candle through endless mazes of rooms and corridors. Finally,

the candle halted at a golden paneled door.

"Your room." The door swung open on oiled hinges, revealing the most beautiful room Lucie had

ever seen.

"For me?" Lucie gaped. The stateroom was magnificent, far nicer than anything she'd seen or even

imagined. Ever. "Shouldn't I be in the servant's quarters with the rest of you?"

"Oh, no." Fleur was adamant. "He was very specific you stay in this particular room."

Lucie heard rustling as Fleur bustled about. Windows flew open, then cupboards, as Fleur laid out a variety of fragrant soaps next to a shiny, copper bath.

"I'll send Louis up to fill this bath," Fleur explained, as an outdated, but luxurious blue velvet dress

soared across the room, spreading itself on the bed. "We can adjust the dresses, but this one should

fit for now. I'll be back in a twinkle. I'm sure you're starving and ready for a nice cup of tea."

"But I'm supposed to work here. There seems to be some misunderstanding. Why are you bringing

tea to my room?" Lucie protested, brow crinkling in confusion.

"Work...?" Fleur's voice trailed off. "Well, never mind, we'll sort it tomorrow after you settle in."

Lucie sank onto the bed, her head spinning. The door clicked shut behind Fleur, leaving Lucie in the

empty and blessedly silent room.

Moments later, her bath arrived. Buckets floated through the air, dumping clean, scalding water into

the tub. Lucie sank into the rose scented water with a sigh of pleasure. Hot baths were not a

frequent luxury in her forest cabin. Usually the best Lucie managed was a rub of harsh soap rinsed

with a dash of cold water at the well.

Lucie wrapped herself in a warm towel, sniffing the whiff of dried lavender clinging to the soft fabric.

She slid into the blue dress Fleur laid out for her. Her old mud-streaked dress had been whisked

away, accompanied by a sniff of displeasure from the disapproving Fleur.

Lucie sat leisurely at the vanity. The mistaken room would surely be discovered soon; she might as

well enjoy herself now. Lucie curled her toes into the satiny slippers Fleur had left her. A size too big,

still, far better than her own pair. Those pinched her feet fiercely every time she put them on.

"Nearly ready for dinner?"

Lucie yelped, nearly falling off the stool when she heard Fleur's eager voice a mere foot away.

"Warn me next time you come in like that. You startled me." Lucie's hand flew to her thudding

heart.

"Sorry," Fleur cheerfully fluffed the bottom of Lucie's outdated dress. "I guess we've been here so

long we're used to being invisible."

"How long? Have you always been at the chateau?" Lucie leaned her elbows on the vanity.

"Oh, I don't know." Fleur's voice was airy. "A few hundred years?"

"A few hundred!" Lucie squeaked, banging her elbows as they slipped off the side of the vanity.

"Why didn't anyone find you?" She rubbed the forming bruise.

"Well, we weren't in this form — exactly," Fleur explained. "I can't explain it to you, I don't know

myself exactly how it happened. An evil magician put us under a curse — trapped us. But when he

came, part of the curse lifted. That's why the chateau returned. The chateau and the grounds were a ruin. We were ... well, we were nothing. Just air, floating particles. I only remember vague pieces of what happened before he freed us." A towel floated over and began briskly rubbing Lucie's damp hair.

"I didn't think curses worked in Lovan," Lucie said, her voice muffled under the towel.

"I guess things have changed then." Fleur said. The towel neatly folded itself onto a nearby rack.

"We haven't been able to leave the chateau grounds. We've tried a few times since he's arrived and can't get past the gates."

"Who is he?" Lucie asked, grimacing as Fleur worked out a stubborn knot in her dark hair.

"Well, we call him Red — Master Red, if we're addressing him." Fleur answered. "He won't — or can't tell us his actual name. And I tried finding out." Fleur lowered her voice to a near whisper; her breath tickling the back of Lucie's neck. "It upsets him — we don't bring it up anymore. In truth, I don't care what Red's name is. We're all so grateful to him." A few pins floated off the vanity, hovering over Lucie's hair before digging into her scalp.

"What about the rest of the curse?" Lucie winced as strands of hair twisted into tight curls.

"We're all just hoping Red breaks the curse. If got this far, he can break the rest. He just needs time."

Fleur's voice was optimistic as she patted Lucie's elaborate hairstyle. "There you're ready for dinner."

"Dinner?" Lucie smoothed velvet ruffles on her dress. She hoped Fleur had a few simpler dresses

tucked in the wardrobe. The dress was so heavy and unwieldy she found it difficult to move.

"I eat dinner in the kitchen with the staff. You're joining Master Red." A soft wrap settled around

Lucie's bare shoulders.

Butterflies swarmed in Lucie's stomach. The anxieties shoved into the darkest corners of her mind

flooded to the surface.

"What's he like — Master Red?" Lucie faltered.

"Well," Fleur hesitated, searching for words. "He's very ... tall."

"Tall? What else?" Lucie narrowed her eyes suspiciously.

"Strong. And he has a good heart. You'll love him once you get to know him."

"A temper then?" Lucie asked, remembering her father's story.

"Not exactly a temper, I think ... just used to having his own way. But really, he's quite lovely. A dear.

Just give him time," Fleur's voice encouraged as she tugged on Lucie's dress, guiding her toward the

door.

"Well, I suppose that's all right." Lucie had dealt with rowdy customers at The Orc's Head. She

followed Fleur out the door, letting the door close silently behind her.

CHAPTER SEVEN

Lucie followed Fleur's candle as it bobbed down the endless labyrinth of passages. I'm going to learn my way around this chateau. It's like a city, Lucie thought, panting as her too big satin slippers slapped against the polished marble.

Finally, Fleur opened a great double door. Lucie followed the candle into the largest dining room she had ever seen. Silver and fine china gleamed from two places set at a table stretching the length of the room. Intricate tapestries and gilt-framed paintings hung from the walls. The setting sun streamed light from tall windows lining one wall.

Lucie straightened her spine, gliding to the one of the chairs. She dragged out the carved wooden chair, cringing as it scraped the polished floor and sat, carefully arranging the folds of her dress around her.

Instantly, the room filled with delicious smells as a parade of plates floated toward her. Lucie gaped at the vast number of dishes crammed on the loaded table. Red must have a giant appetite, she thought, hoping they weren't expecting her to eat it all. Even the finest dinner party Marion had held didn't begin to compare to this.

A gold-rimmed plate of creamy bisque settled in front of her, delicate tendrils of steam curling to the

vast ceiling. In spite of the nerves dancing through her body, Lucie was hungry. She lifted her spoon,

tasting cautiously, the rich salty flavour spread along her tongue. Delicious, Lucie thought as she

relaxed and dug her spoon happily into the bowl.

An enormous figure flung the door open, banging it against the wall. Lucie's spoon froze halfway to

her mouth. A hulking form appeared in her field of vision. Lucie fought back a squeak of fear and

dismay at the sight that appeared before her. The creature was huge. Had Lucie been standing, it

would have towered over her. Wild hair covered faintly human features of the beast's face. If that

wasn't enough, she glimpsed fangs glistening through the russet strands. Covering her alarm, Lucie

schooled her features into what she hoped was a polite smile.

"Good evening," Lucie said. Her voice shook as she averted her gaze, trying not to stare at the

creature. "I hope you don't mind," she said, gesturing toward the soup with a white-knuckled hand.

"I didn't want the soup to get cold. And it smelled so delicious I just couldn't resist."

"Humph." A deep growling voice snorted.

"I'm Lucie." She fidgeted with the spoon, not sure whether to continue eating.

"You can call me Red," the voice grumbled. His chair creaked under his weight as the beast settled.

Lucie took a deep breath, gathering her courage. "I'm wondering. Is there some kind of mistake? I

mean, my father said we were supposed to be doing a term of service. Shouldn't I eat in the kitchen

with the rest of the staff?" Lucie stumbled over words that suddenly felt clumsy in her mouth. No

matter how good the soup was, she preferred Fleur's invisible but cheery company to this miserable

creature.

"No, no mistake." The husky voice was gruff. "I need a term of service." Red reached a giant hairy

claw toward a roll, awkwardly stuffing it in his mouth. Crumbs littered the pristine white tablecloth.

Lucie's eyes skittered away, pretending not to notice his ineptitude.

"What would you like me to perform? I mean, what are my duties?" Lucie leaned back as invisible

hands whisked away her soup, replacing it with another plate.

She poked at it with a fork. It was roast duck. Lucie brought a forkful of the savoury dish, dripping

with rich sauce, to her mouth, closing her eyes blissfully as the flavours exploded on her tongue.

"Duties?" The rumbling voice jerked Lucie back the present.

"Yes, duties." She hastily swallowed the duck and cut another piece.

Red paused before he fisted his taloned hand around a fork and speared a slice of duck, shoving it

into his mouth. "Fleur will cover your duties with you."

"But she said you would tell me," Lucie answered in her most reasonable and pleasant tone. She

watched in fascination as Red swallowed his whole plateful of food without chewing once.

"My, my, you're feisty for such a little thing. I just need someone to send a message for me."

"A message?" Lucie's fork clinked down on the china plate, her mouth rounding in surprise. It baffled

her. If her job was sending a message, why was she in the dining room ... wearing this ridiculous

velvet dress no less?

"Is that so hard to understand?" Red narrowed his eyes, baring his gleaming fangs.

"No, I'm quite happy to be a messenger. But if I'm only a messenger, I was just wondering why I'm in

the dining room with you?" Lucie attempted to be diplomatic as she picked up her fork and prodded

at the next dish.

"Why shouldn't you eat with me? You mean I'm too ugly for you?" his voice rumbled louder,

frustration slashing across his face.

"No, not at all." Lucie protested, her voice weak. "I just thought maybe you needed someone in the

kitchen or maybe the laundry. You know I'm really industrious. I worked in a tavern all last year."

"You don't want the burden of this," Red shouted. He swiped a paw in the air, gesturing at his twisted features. Lucie flinched away from pointed nails waving dangerously through the air. "You

can't stand to even look at me for one second." The rumble was now a roar; one giant fist pounded

the table, the delicate china shivering under the force.

"Let me tell you. I'm not thrilled about this either. But you're not going anywhere. You aren't leaving

until I say so!"

Red's chair crashed to the ground as he flung it back, standing abruptly and storming away. The door

slammed shut behind him, shaking the paintings until they quivered on the wall.

CHAPTER EIGHT

"Fleur?" Lucie hesitantly poked her head around the edge of the door.

Only a faint echo answered. Lucie had waited a reasonable amount of time before deeming it safe to return to her stateroom. After Red's outburst, the invisible servants scattered, the dining room went silent, the food on the table lay cold and forgotten.

"Just wonderful," Lucie muttered, peering down the endless hallway, hoping for a familiar landmark to guide her way.

After wandering miles of corridors, Lucie finally stumbled on the door to her stateroom. Kicking off her slippers, she crawled into bed still wearing the blue velvet dress. Exhaustion claimed her, and she fell into a deep sleep.

Lucie's nose twitched, sensing something warm and delicious nearby. She sat up, shielding her eyes from the bright sunlight streaming through the window.

"Good morning!" Fleur's musical voice greeted her as Lucie sat up.

A breakfast tray floated across the room, settling itself on the bed. A silver dome lifted away to reveal warm, flaky pastries arranged on a china plate. A chubby silver pot poured hot chocolate.

Lucie's stomach growled.

"Morning," Lucie said. She bit into a pastry. Strawberry, sweet tart fruit melted together with warm

buttery pastry in her mouth. She washed it down with a gulp of the hot chocolate.

"I couldn't find you last night," Lucie complained, taking another bite of pastry.

"Sorry, the master — Red was pre-occupied. I'm glad you found your way." Lucie detected a hint of

concern in the invisible voice.

"Eventually," Lucie said. It was hard to feel upset when eating something this delicious. Lucie licked

the last bit of strawberry off buttery fingers, wiping them on a linen cloth.

"Is he always that temperamental? He's very easily offended." Lucie scrunched her nose.

"It's not my place to have an opinion on Red's temper," Fleur said, laying out another dress, just as

puffy and uncomfortable as the blue velvet one. "We'll get these dresses fitted today. I've measured

your old shoes, so those will be ready this afternoon." Fleur sniffed in disapproval at the state of

Lucie's old slippers. "You'll meet Master Red by the east fountain at ten. He walks in the rose garden

after breakfast."

Lucie's mouth drooped. She was hoping to avoid the beast until at least dinner, then send the message with utmost speed so she could leave this place. "Are you sure he wants me to walk with

him? He didn't seem thrilled with my company last night."

"Oh, yes," Fleur tutted when she noticed Lucie wearing last night's dress.

After suffering more of Fleur's fussing and primping, Lucie finally dressed to Fleur's satisfaction.

Fleur led Lucie to a large formal garden, depositing her near a large fountain before rushing off,

muttering about new laces for the dress.

"You're here." She turned, Red strode toward her, wearing an outmoded velvet jacket and matching

breeches. "Let's go."

Red stalked across the lawn toward a spacious greenhouse and Lucie was soon out of breath, trying

to keep up with his long legs.

"Do you always walk this fast?" she puffed.

"Do you always ask this many questions?" Red retorted, amusement in his voice keeping up the brisk

pace.

"I don't think so. It's just everything is strange here. Different. Magic." Lucie paused to catch her

breath, smelling the whiff of rich earth mixed with wet grass and sunshine. Red stopped to glare.

"I've never seen magic before. It's quite impressive. That's what this is, isn't it?" Lucie waved a hand

encompassing the chateau and the gardens.

"Yes," Red grumbled.

"Well, I wouldn't have so many questions if you explained everything to me." Lucie sat down on a stone bench. A breeze rustled through the leaves, cooling her hot cheeks.

Red stared pointedly at the bench, until Lucie scooted over, making space for him.

"You want an explanation?" Red lowered himself, stretching out his legs.

"Yes." Lucie tipped her face toward the sun.

"Fine, I'll explain. I'm cursed. An immensely powerful mage cursed me, and I'm stuck here—like

this—until we break the curse or it wears off on its own."

"Can you break the curse?" Lucie turned, wide-eyed, to search Red's face, overcoming her aversion

to his strange features. His eyes weren't bad, quite human with flecks of gold in the hazel centre.

"I don't know." The bench creaked ominously as Red leaned back. "From what I know, every curse

has an escape, but I'm no mage and I've tried everything."

"Nothing's impossible," Lucie scoffed, pity making her brave. "Is that why I'm here, to help break the

curse? I could ride for help. From what I've heard, Princess Penelope from Iaisa is a very powerful

mage. Maybe I could take her a message and she'll help." Lucie babbled, unnerved at Red's

proximity.

"Never speak that name in my presence again," Red growled, venom in his voice.

"Why? Is she the mage who cursed you?" The words rushed out of Lucie's mouth before she could

pull them back.

Lucie cringed as Red leapt up, pacing back and forth. Red's face twisted in rage.

"Don't speak of her!" he shouted, flinging his arm out, nearly backhanding Lucie. Instead, he

whacked his hand on the edge of the bench with a thud.

"I'm sorry!" She scrambled back, horrified at Red's fierce expression. "I didn't mean to offend."

"Offend me? You didn't mean to offend me?" Red thundered. He clutched his hand, grunting in pain.

"Do you think I'm blind as well as ugly? I saw your face at dinner. Do you think I want this face?"

"No, of course not." Lucie's attempts to soothe the irate Red fell flat. "I was just trying to help."

"Get out of my sight," he said. The leaves trembled with the force of Red's roar.

Terrified, Lucie turned on her heel and ran.

CHAPTER NINE

Lucie crashed through trees and underbrush, branches tearing at her skirts as she stumbled over
rough ground. She veered around a thornbush, her heart pounding violently as the stitch in her side
intensified.

After hours in the forest, she no longer knew which direction she was going, and judging by the
lengthening shadows, it was late afternoon. Lucie paused, searching for a way to orient herself.

Colossal oak trees stretched endlessly in every direction, their thick branches and dense leaves
creating shifting patterns on the forest floor.

Lucie wished desperately she had paid attention to the scenery when Fleur led her to the chateau.

There must be a landmark, she thought, a path or a stream, even a distinctive boulder to mark the
way. Lucie scrambled down a ravine, vaguely recalling hunters in the Orc's Head following brooks
when they lost their bearings.

"Now, how do I find a brook?" she muttered, wishing she had paid more attention to the
conversation when offered the chance.

She took a few faltering steps toward a promising stand of trees, then froze. A howl split the air.

Wolves. Lucie swung around as another howl answered from the opposite direction.

Lucie sprinted to the closest tree, scrabbling at a low branch and swinging up just as a mangy grey

wolf slunk menacingly toward her through the under-brush. Lucie frantically clawed to a higher

branch. She clung to the branch in dismay; staring as three companions joined the wolf. The wolves

circled the tree, sniffing and pawing at the ground under-neath Lucie's perch.

Lucie had heard rumours about wolves entering Lovan, but never dreamed she might see one. The

wolves were huge, their rangy bodies standing nearly the height of her shoulder. Their sharp teeth

gleamed fiercely as they whined, settling underneath her tree, yelping occasionally as they looked

up at her branch.

Hours later, Lucie shivered as the branch creaked danger-ously in the wind. The wolves were restless;

they paced and whimpered. Finally, the largest male wolf sat under her tree, threw his head back

and gave a bone-chilling howl. It was then that it hap-pened.

Trees shook with a booming roar as a vast hairy figure lunged toward the skulking animals. It was

Red. He snatched the biggest wolf by the scruff of the neck and shook viciously, sending it crashing to the ground with a groan. The other wolves leapt on Red. Lucie bit her fist as he disappeared into a

whirlwind of growling teeth and fur.

Lucie bit back a cry of horror as a female wolf sank jagged fangs into Red's shoulder. He slammed her

into the ground and she limped away, yelping. Soon the two remaining wolves joined her, scattering

into the murky shadows. Spent, Red slumped under the tree, cradling his wounds.

Cautiously, Lucie crept down from her branch, scraping her arm on the rough bark as she clumsily

tumbled in a heap on the ground.

"Are you all right?" She stumbled to Red, anxiously examining the worst of his injuries.

He moaned, blood dripping through fingers that clutched his injured shoulder. Lucie used her teeth

to tear a strip off the bottom of her underskirt, using it to tie up a deep cut on his leg. It was

impossible to wrap the shoulder, so Lucie wadded up the fabric, pressing it on the wound. The other

injuries would have to wait.

"Can you stand?" Lucie asked, biting her lip. There was no way Lucie could support Red's weight. She

couldn't leave him there, not with darkness falling and the threat of the wolves' return.

"I think so," Red said. He heaved to his feet, swaying as he fought to regain balance.

"Lean on me," she said. Lucie braced herself as he put one heavy arm around her shoulder. A smear

of blood drew a line across the sleeve of her dress.

The pair awkwardly shuffled through the forest, pausing often to rest. Red weighed heavier and heavier on Lucie's slight shoulders; her back ached from the effort of holding him up.

Darkness fell, and Lucie had to depend on Red's superior eyesight to guide them over the rough ground. Relief flooded her exhausted body as the warm lights of the Chateau came into view. They stumbled up the steps and through the front entrance.

The chateau was immediately in an uproar as a cluster of voices gathered around their beloved Master Red.

"Fleur, get me warm water and bandages. And you," Lucie gestured at a young-sounding male voice.

"Louis," the voice said.

"Louis, help Master Red to his room. He'll need bandaged; bring ointment if you have it," Lucie commanded.

Lucie took charge with an air of authority. In a scurry of footsteps, the servants moved to do her bidding. Trailing mud and dried leaves, Lucie and Red limped to his apartments, where Lucie efficiently made herself at home. Lucie hoped she could remember how Althea patched up injuries as she dipped the cloth in warm water to clean the wound on Red's shoulder.

"We'll keep an eye on this cut," Lucie murmured, wringing out the cloth and patting the wound.

"Ow!" Red gritted his teeth as Lucie unravelled the cloth wrapped around his leg.

"Stay still, I need to check the wound," she told him. Lucie carefully moved Red's foot from side to

side, squinting at the bite wounds.

"I may have to stitch it," she remarked. Red groaned in response, clenching his bedclothes tight.

With needle, thread and other implements fetched by the Fleur, Lucie sewed the wound carefully.

"I'm very glad you came after me," she said. Lucie snipped the end of the thread, applying a strong-

smelling ointment to the wound. Ignoring his groans and complaints, she spread the yellow paste

liberally over his skin. "Especially after I upset you."

"Of course," Red winced as her hand brushed a tender bruise. "I shouldn't have lost my temper like

that. I've no excuse, I'm just not used to being this—this thing." He grimaced, spreading out his

hands and glaring at the long nails.

"You couldn't have fought the wolves without the curse," Lucie reminded Red as she covered the

wound with a light bandage. She adjusted the stack of pillows piled behind him.

"Well," Red hesitated. "I suppose you're right." Silenced by her observation, his eyes followed her as

she completed her tasks and left the room.

CHAPTER TEN

Lucie watched, fascinated. Flour and sugar flew through the air and whisked into a mixing bowl. Eggs cracked and a sticky ball of dough formed under invisible hands.

"Did you need something, dear?" The voice was older, a motherly woman, by Lucie's best guess.

"Hello, Maribel. I thought I'd take some soup to Red if you have any in the pot." Determined to help Red heal, Lucie made every effort to keep Red in bed. He was proving to be a difficult patient, restless and energetic at best, downright impatient at worst.

"You're too late. He's practicing. Look outside in the courtyard," Maribel said.

Without a hitch, the dough kneaded itself on the kitchen table, forming small balls that would later become Maribel's delicious sweet rolls.

Lucie peered out the kitchen door. There he was, Red, sword in hand, a resolute expression on his face. Despite the limp, he flew around the courtyard, parrying, striking and lunging in a deadly dance of one. Unnoticed, Lucie stared for a moment. Even to her unpracticed eye, he was clearly unmatched in strength and speed.

He caught her eye, then stumbled, slipping on a loose stone. Lucie ran to catch him, staggering

under his weight as they crashed to the cobblestones.

"What do you think you're doing? You have to heal," Lucie scolded as Red righted himself, rubbing

his wounded leg.

"I can't be weak right now. I need to make sure I'm pre-pared."

"Prepared for what? It's just us in the chateau," Lucie said. She stood back as he brushed himself off.

"Maybe now," Red replied, "but someday, I'm leaving this chateau. And when I leave, I'll be ready –

ready to meet the one who cursed me." Red stepped back into position, raising the sword.

Frightened by the venom colouring Red's voice, Lucie re-treated a few steps. Without a beat, he

began again. Striking, parrying, lunging. Resolute. Seeing Red's determination, Lucie retreated to the

kitchen, closing the door softly behind her.

At dinner that evening, Lucie picked at her fish. Alone. Lucie felt strangely relieved when the door

banged open and Red limped across the dining room. Red healed with astonishing speed. Red pulled

out the heavy chair, easing himself into it.

"Will we look for a way to break the curse tomorrow?" Lucie picked carefully at her fish, examining

each bite for any stray bones.

"I suppose." Red balanced his food on his fork, muttering an oath when it splattered onto the white

tablecloth.

"Where should we start?" Lucie took a cautious bite, savouring the lemony tang from the sauce cook

had put on it.

Red paused, a half-eaten roll in his hand. "We can start in the library," he said.

"You have a library here?" Lucie squeaked in excitement. When her father lost his business, she,

much to her regret, was forced to sell all, but the most tattered, of her beloved books.

Red nodded. "Do you like to read?"

"I love books," she said as she squeezed lemon on her asparagus. She took a bite. "In my house,

before we moved, I read all the time."

She finished the asparagus and moved her attention to a sweet bun, inhaling the smell of cinnamon

and cloves before nibbling at the icing. "When can we go?"

"Now," he said. Red stuffed the rest of his roll into his mouth. "Let's go."

Red led Lucie all the way to the west tower, a part of the chateau Lucie hadn't explored. After

climbing a twisting staircase, they arrived at a large wooden door.

"Can I open it?" Lucie asked Red, giving him a hesitant look that he answered with a nod.

Lucie sneezed as the wonderful, dusty, unmistakable smell of books assaulted her nose. Lots of

books.

"Unbelievable!" Lucy gaped at rows of books stretching out in every direction.

She ran a hand along the spine of a gold-edged volume, then craned her neck up gaze up at rows of

books, ascending to ceiling height. There was a clever wooden balcony along with several

stepladders allowing access to the tall shelves.

"I don't know where to start," she said, examining the titles on a nearby shelf. Some of these books

aren't even written in Lavonian. We can't possibly get through them all."

"It's organized in sections," Red explained. "Or at least my library at home is. We start at either the

history or magic section and go from there."

"This would be easier if the writing wasn't completely archaic," Lucie complained, squinting at a

page of slanted script. "As far as I can see, this section is novels and fairy tales."

She glanced at Red, who was trying not to tear the fragile books with his clawed fingers.

After days of searching, Lucie wondered if they would ever find something useful. She set down her

book, stretching.

"I'm going to see what's in that corner," she said.

Lucie gestured at a yet unexplored corner of the room. Red glanced up from where he sprawled

against a cushioned seat, legs propped up on a cushioned footstool.

Lucie pulled out a chunky volume of fairy tales, with a picture of a gold lion prancing along the front

cover.

"Wait, a minute. I think I might have found something." Excitement coloured her voice.

"Bring it here. I'm too comfortable to move," Red said. He set aside the book he was rifling through

and held out a lazy hand.

"No, not the book, the shelf," she said.

Lucie took more books from the shelf and piled them into a neat stack on a side table. Red jumped

up to join Lucie, peering at the back of the shelf.

"I've seen something like this before – a hidden door. Stand back a moment, I'll see if I can get it

open," he said.

He reached back to the small lever Lucie had discovered and scrabbled, trying to get his fingers

underneath the pulling mechanism. "I can't quite grasp it; my nails are too long." He glared at the

offending hands in frustration.

"Here, let me." Lucie put her hand around the small lever and gave it a sharp tug. They stood back as

silently, slowly, the entire shelf of books swung open.

CHAPTER ELEVEN

Acrid dust billowed from the hidden chamber, clouding their vision, making their eyes water and sting. When the dust cleared, Lucie stepped forward, peering inside. The room wasn't dark as she expected. One window cast a dim glow across the stone floor.

"Empty storage space," she said. Disappointed, Lucie stood aside to let Red look.

"Wait. What's that?" Red pointed out a grimy tapestried drape, covering one entire wall.

"An old curtain?" Lucie crinkled her nose. She hovered outside the doorway. Strange prickling sensations washed over her skin and seemed to be emanating from the mysterious room.

"Yes, but, what's behind the curtain?" Red strode inside, dust flying with each footstep.

He swept the tapestry aside, revealing an immense gold-framed mirror. Cold. Gleaming. Rays of light bounced off its polished surface, scattering prisms on the stone floor.

"Oh!" Captivated, Lucie drifted toward the mirror. "Beautiful." She peered at the design carved into the ornate frame. "Jewels."

"The Lovanian crest," Red said. He pointed to a design tracing the top of the mirror. "If this is what I

think it is, it's truly magical. Something we lost centuries ago."

"Why? What is it?" Lucie slid questioning eyes to Red.

"Originally, each of the five magic kingdoms owned a mirror and scepter. They were, or rather are,

extremely powerful items used to rule the kingdoms. During the War of Destruction, the scepter and

the mirror disappeared. They taught me we destroyed them. I've seen pictures of the mirror and the

scepter, I'd recognize them anywhere. This is that mirror." Excitement danced in Red's eyes.

"You think it's the Lavonian mirror?" Lucie narrowed her eyes, leaning forward, staring the

shimmering glass. "Why would the mirror reappear after centuries? Do you think it still works?"

"I don't know." Red narrowed his eyes, determined. "We can test it."

"How?" Lucie said. A prickle of apprehension ran up her spine. Something in Red's tone told her this

would be a dangerous undertaking.

"The mirror is a tool. It shows you places and people far away."

"How does it work?" she asked.

"It needs to be someone or somewhere familiar, somewhere you can picture in your mind. You

imagine it, ask the mirror, and it appears. The old kings used to spy on their courtiers this way. No

one dared double-cross them."

Lucie reached a curious finger out, stroking the golden frame. To her surprise, a sharp tingle ran up

her arm in response. She jerked her hand back.

"It stung me!" Lucie cradled her smarting hand under her arm.

"It's dangerous," warned Red, "stand back, and I'll see if it works for me."

Lucie stepped back, letting Red concentrate on the mirror.

"Show me King Erich," Red spoke in a commanding voice.

The glossy surface clouded; a fog crept across the mirror's surface, clearing to reveal a formal

garden. A tall man strode across smooth grass toward a laughing golden-haired girl.

"Amazing." Lucie let out the breath she had been holding. "Can I try?"

"Yes, but don't touch it," he said. Red stood aside, allowing Lucie access to the mirror.

"Show me Marion," Lucie said, focused on the mirror.

Again, the surface clouded before clearing to reveal Marion in a domestic scene. She was sitting at

the rickety, old table peeling potatoes. A movement behind her revealed Pierre entering the cabin.

He was smiling and holding up a large basket of apples.

Lucie swallowed hard, blinking back sudden tears of longing and homesickness springing to her eyes.

"They look well. Can I request another scene?" she asked.

"Certainly." Red waited patiently while Lucie gathered control.

Lucie closed her blue eyes, imagining Katherine and whispered her name. This time as the murkiness cleared, the polished surface showed Katherine sitting at her loom, weaving. The rhythmic thud of

the shuttle swung back and forth as Katherine concentrated on the loom.

She's thinner, Lucie thought, watching the steady cadence of Katherine's hand and feet.

"Thank you." Lucie turned to Red, wiping her cheek with the back of her hand.

"Did that upset you?" Red asked.

"I'm not sad," Lucie crossed her arms tightly across her chest. "These are happy tears. I'm just glad

they're safe ... happy. Marion was ill before I left. And things weren't good for Father's business."

"What happened?" Sympathy shone from Red's eyes. He reached to touch Lucie on the shoulder,

then reconsidering, stuffed the hand in his pocket.

"Father's a merchant with three caravans. Over two years, all three caravans vanished. Just poof,

gone, with no sign of them anywhere. Father travelled up and down the trade route searching many

times. It was like they never existed. Before Father lost the caravans, he borrowed money to build

up the business — for us girls. He tried to pay the money back, but it was too much. People were

angry."

A sober look crossed Red's face as he listened intently. "I see."

Lucie shook her head. "It's so strange. An attack from bandits or wild animals would leave signs of a struggle or at least some trail leading to survivors, but Father found nothing. He lost everything

replacing what he owed the merchants. And Marion — my oldest sister. She suffered most; she

cared for Katherine and I. Our mother died when we were young — just babies. She was a second

mother to us. When we moved, it was a shock to her. She became very ill a few months later and

hasn't recovered."

Lucie lowered her eyes and plucked at her embroidered skirt. "Marion was the toast of the town;

engaged to the mercantile owner's son. But father had borrowed money from the mercantile, they

lost the business. That ended the engagement. It broke poor Marion's heart." Lucie finished her tale

with a sigh.

"We'll use the mirror to find out what happened to your father's caravan. If only I could leave the

chateau, I could help," Red said, his eyes narrowing in frustration.

"Thank you, and don't worry, we'll break the curse and get you out of here," Lucie said.

Grateful for Red's understanding, Lucie put her hand on his arm and looked into his eyes without

flinching.

"You don't know what this means to me. It's the first time I've been able to talk to someone about

it."

More determined than ever to help Red break the curse, Lucie gave the mirror one last glance before leaving the mysterious room behind.

CHAPTER TWELVE

Lucie tossed and turned, blankets twisting into a ball around her ankles as she attempted to find a comfortable position. Giving up, she wrapped a warm robe around her shoulders. Slipping out of the stateroom, Lucie crept down twisting corridors. The library door creaked and Lucie's candle flickered as she fumbled for the latch to the hidden door.

"Show me Marion," Lucie said.

She closed her eyes, gathering her thoughts. Slowly the fog cleared, revealing her sister. Lucie stared, shocked. It was clear Marion had relapsed over the past few days. She was more ill than ever.

Father sat by Marion's side, holding her hand. Marion shivered violently, coughing, and Lucie noticed how thin Father had become since she left. Was he even eating at all? Lucie wondered as she saw his clothes hang off his bony frame.

"Show me, Katherine," Lucie demanded.

The scene faded, a new one took its place. Katherine, sobbing into her hands as a pained Mary stood by her side. Mary shook her head sadly, turning away. Unable to tear herself away, Lucie kept watching, glued to the scene.

After a few minutes, Katherine gathered herself, wiping her eyes as she packed up her meager

belongings. She took the path outside Annecy toward the cabin.

What brought this on? Lucie wondered. Mary and Katherine had always been close, bonding over

their shared love of fabrics and textiles. Lucie knew for a fact Mary was setting Katherine up to be

lead weaver next year. Why would she turn away from her protege? Lucie wrapped her arms around

herself, leaving the mirror in silence.

In spite of glorious sunshine streaming through the window and an extra buttery and delicious

pastry, Lucie couldn't raise even a ghost of a smile next morning. Her eyes were red rimmed and

heavy with lack of sleep and her brain felt numb, exhausted from considering every possibility of

how to aid her sisters and her father.

"What's wrong?" asked Red, watching her tear her pastry into tiny crumbs on her plate.

"Nothing. It's fine." Lucie heaved a sigh, toying with the handle of her cup.

"Nothing always means something," insisted Red, shovelling a heaping spoonful of scrambled eggs into his mouth.

"Maybe it's something I can help with."

"It's my family, I watched them in the mirror last night," answered Lucie glumly. "Marion's sick

again. I don't think they're eating properly . And Katherine, I don't know exactly what happened, but

it looked like Mary forced her to leave the weavers."

The whole sad story poured out as Lucie slumped back in her chair.

"I just wish I could help," Lucie finished, picking up a croissant, then setting it down again.

"Do you? So you want to return home?" asked Red. He stirred his coffee, setting the spoon down with a clunk. "I mean, we've been searching the mirror every day, and it's not like we're making progress."

Lucie twisted the butter knife as she held it in her hand.

"There's nothing for me in Annecy. I didn't exactly leave on good terms with everybody and I won't leave the chateau until we break the curse."

"Go for a visit," suggested Red. "It's not like this chateau is going anywhere; take care of your sisters, then return in a few weeks. The curse can wait." Red took a sip of coffee, winced at the bitter taste then added cream and sugar.

Lucie hesitated. "But, what about the wolves?"

"We can go as far as the main road with you, they won't bother you there. Wolves stick to the forest. Louis and I will keep you safe. Once you reach the path, you can go on by yourself. We have much more than we need at the chateau, I'll send things with you — things to help them get back on their feet. I don't know why I didn't think of it before." He took a sip of coffee, smiling encouragingly.

Lucie beamed. "Really?" she squealed, joyfully leaping up to give Red a big hug. He froze for a moment before putting an arm gently around her shoulder, squeezing cautiously.

Blackie's saddlebags clinked, laden with coins, spices, and all kinds of other things that Red, with

prodding and encouragement from Fleur, insisted were necessary for Lucie's family. The entire staff

showed up to see her off. Invisible voices cheerily wished her luck as they gathered to send Lucie

through the King's Forest.

Red and Louis accompanied Lucie to the verge of the vast property.

"I'll miss you." Red swallowed, hazel eyes darkening.

"I'll miss you too," Lucie said. She searched Red's face, surprised at finding her words were true.

"But, I am coming back, you know. You won't get rid of me that easily."

With a wave, Lucie was off, disappearing in a sea of green light.

The trip was smooth, quiet, but apprehension gripped Lucie as she drew near Annecy, crossing the

stone bridge edging the village. After the debacle at the Orc's Head, Lucie assumed Annecy wouldn't

welcome her with open arms.

Knowing Blanchette's reputation for gossip and twisting a story to suit her own purposes, she would

be very unwelcome. Lucie glued her gaze to Blackie's ears; ignoring stares and mutters as Blackie

trotted down the cobblestone street, past the market square.

It was market day. People crowded the street, bustling with venders and shoppers alike. By

suppertime, word of Lucie's return would have circulated through every house in Annecy. Her

shoulders sagged with relief as she finally left Annecy behind her, heading down the forest path

toward the cabin.

"Lucie?" Katherine froze, shocked as Blackie jingled his way into the small clearing, polished bridle

winking in the sunlight. "Is it really you?"

She dropped the bucket she was holding, spilling water over her shoes. Katherine ignored the muddy

circle spreading around her, gaping open-mouthed.

"It's me!" Lucie slid off the saddle, embracing Katherine. "I'm home."

Tears of joy and relief spilled from Katherine's eyes as she squeezed her sister tightly. "We thought

you were dead." She wept. "When Father told me about the beast, and showed me the note you

left, I was terrified."

"I did go to Red — the beast," explained Lucie. "But he's very kind to me. He sent me to help you

immediately when we found out you were in trouble."

Katherine sighed, leaning down to pick up her fallen bucket. "Things are bad," she confided.

"Marion's tincture ran out, and she's taken a turn for the worse."

"And Father, well, let's say the town hasn't forgotten what happened. No one will give him work anywhere. Blanchette's telling wild tales about you. She said you tried to steal Henri's silver. Half the

town believes her too. Ridiculous! People should know better than to believe Blanchette! We knew

the truth, of course." Katherine's lip trembled, she hesitated.

"But Mary had to send me home. People threatened to pull their orders." A tear glittered on

Katherine's eyelash.

Lucie huffed as she removed Blackie's bridle and unsaddled him.

"Of course I didn't steal Henri's silver. That was Bridgette being Bridgette. She put it in my apron

pocket and pretended I stole it. And you know Henri. He's sensible; but when it comes to Blanchette,

she can do nothing wrong."

Lucie led Blackie to the well and dipped out a bucket; letting him drink his fill.

"It left us in quite a predicament though, and when you disappeared it, just fuelled the fire. That's

why so many people do think you stole Henri's money," Katherine said.

A pang of guilt stabbed Lucie. She should have realised Annecy would take out its suspicions on her

father and sisters.

"I'm sorry. But I had to leave. Things would have been worse if I stayed in Annecy," Lucie protested.

She jumped back when Blackie blew into the water, sending a shower of droplets spraying over her

dress.

"I understand why you left," Katherine said, brushing stray drops of water off her dress. "I blame

Blanchette. Not you."

She trailed behind as Lucie led Blackie to a promising patch of grass behind the carrot patch, leaving

him to graze.

"Things will be better now. Red is good to me. Kind. He wants to help. Look." Lucie proudly reached

over Katherine, opening Blackie's saddlebag. She removed a hefty bag of coins. "He sent you this. It

should last you ages."

Katherine picked up a heavy coin and held it up to the light; turning it back and forth to examine the

inscriptions on it. "What are these coins? How did he even get them?"

"Red gave them to me, I suppose they must have been in the Chateau when he arrived. Do you think

we'll be able to use them?"

"Hmm ... very generous of him," Katherine said. She let the coin fall back into the pouch. Begrudging

admiration shone from her eyes. "I suppose if he wanted to help, he might not so terrible."

"No, Father was mistaken about him. He's not really even a beast; he's a person who happens to be

under a curse. I know that sounds strange, even impossible; after all, we are in Lovan. But Red wants

to help me — us. And I — I want to help him. That's the real reason I stayed so long. I was hoping to

help him break the curse." Lucie took the pouch and pulled the drawstring tight, returning it to the saddlebag.

"Well, that may be, but in Father's eyes, he's a beast." Katherine ushered Lucie toward the rickety

front door.

"Maybe, but he's my beast," Lucie muttered under her breath, stepping over the threshold into the

dimly lit cabin.

She strained her eyes through the gloomy haze, furrowing her brow in concern as Marion struggled

to a sitting position. Things were worse than she thought, much worse. Marion's pale face and

wasted flesh shone waxy under the dismal light that filtered through the faded curtains. Her skin

stretched across her cheekbones, so fragile it was nearly translucent. Lucie rushed to Marion's side.

"I've missed you!" she cried as she gingerly embraced her sister. The delicate bones of Marion's

spine dug into her fingertips.

"Red sent me something for you," Lucie told Marion.

She then turned toward Katherine. "In the inner side pocket of that saddlebag there's a packet of

herbs. Put the kettle on and I'll mix some in the tea," Lucie instructed.

"We don't have tea," Marion said, her voice rattling through the small cabin.

"Right. Just boil the kettle then. We'll worry about tea later."

As soon the kettle boiled over the fire Lucie had stoked, she poured the scalding water over the

herbs she had measured out. She breathed in deeply as the rich scent of cloves and cinnamon tickled
her nose.

The spoon clinked against the cup as Lucie swirled the mixture, then brought the cup to Marion.

Propping her up against the lumpy pillows, she tenderly spooned the mixture into Marion's mouth.

When the cup was nearly empty, Marion leaned back with a sigh, closing her eyes.

"What about Father?" Lucie whispered to Katherine as she covered Marion with a blanket.

"He's gone into the woods to forage."

"Poaching?" Lucie's voice rose. Poaching was a serious offense, if caught. "Isn't there food growing
in the garden? When I left, the garden was full. Surely there're vegetables left? What happened to
the potatoes?" Lucie set the cup and spoon down and looked around the small kitchen, noticing bare
shelves and cupboards.

"We have a few carrots and a couple of turnips. Our potatoes didn't grow this year, died right in the
ground. Then the deer ate the other vegetables. We tried everything; but they just kept coming
back. We gathered some food before the deer ate it all," Katherine said.

"With things the way they are in Annecy, we've had to eat it. I sold apples at the market and traded
some to Althea for the tincture. Then people were angry when Father returned and they wouldn't

buy anything from us. The only person in Annecy on our side was Althea. I couldn't put her in a

dangerous position in the village, so I kept my distance. Althea depends on Annecy to make her

living."

Lucie nodded, her eyes thoughtful. Lucie didn't know what happened in other towns but Annecy

residents held grudges. They had a long memory in this tiny village. A single bad choice or unsavoury

bit of gossip could be someone's downfall.

"I have a plan," Lucie said as she rummaged through the cupboard, pulling out the carrots and

turnip. She carefully pulled out the rickety chair and sat at the scarred kitchen table to peel and slice

them.

"I've got enough coins here for you, Marion and Father to move to another town - somewhere far

away where you can start over." Lucie put the carrots and turnip in a metal pot and added water,

salt and pepper.

"A change of scenery and good food will do wonders for Marion. At nightfall, I'll go to Althea's, she

has a garden and enough trade. She'll have food to last us until the next town – somewhere not on

Father's old caravan route." Lucie said. She frowned as she hung the pot over the fire, stirring the

mixture with a wooden spoon.

"Unfortunately, everyone in Annecy knows I'm here. They saw me and Blackie ride through town, but the less I show my face the better. You know how people get when they're antagonised.

Remember what happened with the blacksmith?" Lucie added more salt to the pot.

Katherine raised an eyebrow. "Ian? But he got caught with the baker's daughter. It's hardly the same

thing. You didn't actually do anything wrong."

Lucie sat in the wooden chair. "Yes, but they don't know that. I wouldn't want to get Blanchette

stirred up again. You know Liliana will follow whatever she says. Once word spreads round The Orc's

Head, there's no telling what will happen," Lucie said.

"We'll just have to lie low until Marion feels well enough to travel, then start fresh. Maybe we'll

head west. That's the opposite direction from Father's old caravan routes. Who knows, if we save up

and we're careful, Father could start another caravan. It will be small, but he'll build it up again.

That's what Red thinks anyway," Lucie added.

Katherine wrinkled her nose at the casual tone Lucie used to speak about Red.

Ignoring Katherine, Lucie continued: "You can start weaving again, you know you're good enough to

set up your own looms. Marion can sew; she loves that." Her face brightened as she mapped out

possibilities.

"What about you? What will you do?" Katherine asked her sister.

Lucie faltered. "I'm going back to the chateau."

"What?" Katherine asked, aghast. She picked up the broom, sweeping furiously.

"I'm going back to help Red. Until we break the curse." Lucie set her mouth in a stubborn line.

"But, why can't you just come with us?" Katherine pleaded, scattering piles of dust with her vigorous

sweeping. "I'll admit he's generous. Too generous, if you ask me. But you can't waste your life on a

curse. I mean, what if you never break the curse? Are you going to live in that crumbling chateau for

the rest of your life?"

"I promised Red I'd help," Lucie said simply, her eyes filling with determination. "I promised him I'd

come back after two weeks."

"I can't believe you'd go back. I mean, what if you get caught? You know what the penalty is for

consorting with magic. And this is big magic, even compared to Iasia."

"I'm going to help him." Lucie crossed her arms stubbornly, ignoring the puffs of dust Katherine was

raising.

Katherine rolled her eyes, setting the broom down. "I think you're making a big mistake, but if that's

what you want, I'll help you. But, you're going to have to tell Father yourself."

Later, Lucie left the little cabin, slipping through Annecy under the velvety darkness. A twinge of

regret squeezed her heart as she passed their old house, lying empty, ivy-covered walls looming proudly behind the wrought-iron gate. When Lucie reached Althea's modest cottage, she made her

way up the path, inhaling the scent of lavender and rosemary wafting fresh and clean through the

damp night air.

"I've been waiting for you," Althea said.

She opened the door just as Lucie raised her hand to knock. The older woman pulled Lucie inside,

checking to make sure no curious neighbours were watching. Althea drew Lucie into the warm, cosy

room, where a crackling fire chased away the evening chill.

"You have?" Lucy asked. She loosened the cloak she was clutching tightly around her shoulders.

"Of course, my dear. You know I monitor you and your sisters. Just because I don't join in Annecy's

gossip doesn't mean I don't hear it." Althea gestured for Lucie to sit in a cushioned chair by the fire.

"I was wondering if could you trade a few things with me," Lucie asked falteringly. "I couldn't go to

the market. Not when..."

"Of course," Althea spoke soothingly as she poured some fresh mint tea. "What do you need, dear?"

"Enough food to last this week. Whatever you can spare. I have coins, I can pay you," Lucie replied,

gratefully taking the mug of tea Althea held out to her. "And more tincture for Marion. We've run

out, and she relapsed."

"I think I can manage that, my dear," Althea smiled.

Althea busied herself bustling around her small, well-stocked kitchen and soon had a brimming basket ready for Lucie, a freshly baked loaf of bread peeking out of the checkered cloth she laid over

the top. She tucked in raisin cakes and began mixing the tincture.

"The town was certainly in an uproar when you left. Blanchette caused quite the stir with wild

accusations." She ground leaves with her mortar and pestle. "They thought you ran off with a

soldier, after trying to take all Henri and Izzie's savings. Obviously, I knew better—it's surprising what

people will believe these days."

Lucie gasped, splashing hot tea on her lap. "Run off with a soldier? That's the most ridiculous thing

I've ever heard. I would never do that."

"I know you wouldn't," Althea said. She thinned her lips, grinding her pestle into a mixture with

force. "It didn't help when the soldier's were attacked by a wild animal right after you left. Of course,

they blamed you for that too. That's when everyone in Annecy joined in. They ostracised your poor

sister at the market, no one would go near her. I tried to help, but Katherine's far too proud to take

anything from me."

Althea shook her head sadly, tearing leaves from a hanging bunch of herbs and adding them to her

mortar. Lucie clenched small fists together tightly, her chest burned with indignation.

"I saw wolves as well, but how are the wolves my fault? I have no control over them," Lucie said.

Althea gave Lucie an apologetic look. "The wolves made people tense. They're getting closer ...

bolder. Everyone's nervous and they need someone to blame. They accused you of being a mage

because your mother was Iasian."

"And they blamed me." Lucie set her half-drunk cup of tea on the hearth.

"Well, they had help," Althea explained.

"Blanchette." Lucie's eyes glittered. It was so unfair. Blanchette had everything. A mother and father

who adored her, a comfortable home, a pretty face. Why did she have to take everything from Lucie

and her sisters?

"Yes. She was the main instigator. But you know, I believe in you and, I'm always here if you need

me. People will come to their senses, eventually; they know what she's like." Althea's gnarled fingers

patted Lucie soothingly. "You take care of yourself, my dear — until the next time I see you."

Lucie paused in the doorway, soaking in the warm glow surrounding Althea's slight frame, then

slipped down the path toward the cabin.

Lucie would have made it home safely, if it hadn't been for the party of soldiers. They spilled out of

the mouth of the Orc's Head just as Lucie tiptoed past.

Lucie slid back, pressing herself against the wall of the butcher's shop, hoping to blend into the

shadows so the soldiers would pass without notice. Her plan almost worked, until one of the men, eyes not used to the darkness, stumbled over a rough cobblestone, dropping his sword with a

clatter. As he knelt to pick it up, his eyes locked with Lucie's.

"Hello, miss," he leered, drawing the attention of his rowdy companions.

The blood drained from Lucie's face. It was one thing to deal with unruly customers in the tavern

where Henri kept an eagle eye on his customers. But here on the deserted street it was an entirely

different matter. Lucie faltered back as he staggered closer – close enough for her to smell his warm,

foul breath. By now, his companions realised what was happening.

"I remember you. You were barmaid in the Orc's Head before." A familiar face smirked at her, eyes

gleaming in a stray beam of light.

Lucie's pulse sped, her body numb with fear. Michel.

"I heard they dismissed you. Not so high and mighty now, are we?" Michel's sneering voice was

triumphant.

The chill of fear crept up Lucie's spine, numbing her body as he crowded her against the wall. Lucie

took a deep breath, preparing to scream, but a dirty, calloused hand stopped her, clamping over her

mouth like a trap.

It was now or never. Praying Michel was as tipsy as he looked, Lucie shoved him as hard as she

could. Michel stumbled and lost his footing. This was enough for Lucie to dart around him, spinning away as he grabbed her cloak. It jerked from her neck, coming loose in his hand.

Michel howled after her, grasping the cloak uselessly in grubby hands. One of the men gave chase,

but Lucie was faster. Feet scrabbling on loose stones, she skidded across the street, flinging herself

into the very place she had been desperate to avoid. As she tore headlong through the door of The

Orc's Head, her skirt caught on a rough edge of the doorframe and she tumbled. Her basket of

precious food now spilling cracked eggs and scattering raisin cake crumbs all around her.

"Lucie?"

Dazed, Lucie rubbed the painful lump on her head, taking in the chaos surrounding her. She wiped a

smear of egg yolk from her crumpled skirt, before she looked up, locking eyes with her former best

friend.

"What are you doing here?" Liliana sniffed, peering down her nose at Lucie.

Think, Lucie told herself, forcing her thumping heart to slow its breakneck pace. Her mind scrambled

for a suitable answer. By now, Lucie's dramatic entry had gained her plenty of unwanted attention.

Heads turned, inquisitive faces brimming with questions. Henri and Izzie rushed from the kitchen to

investigate the commotion.

"I'm just passing through, I promise," Lucie stammered to the stern-faced Henri who loomed over her. Clearly Blanchette's scheming and whispering had convinced him of her guilt. His eyes were

hard and angry. Henri took her firmly by the arm, pulling her roughly to her feet.

"What is the meaning of this? I told you to stay away," Henri demanded, as Lucie attempted to

straighten her dishevelled appearance.

"I was passing by. I went to get food," Lucie said. Her cheeks flamed with fierce humiliation as she

pointed at the surrounding wreckage. "It's not for me; it's for my Marion and Katherine. If you let

me go, I'll be out of your way. I've found work elsewhere, so I'm not staying in Annecy." She lifted

pleading eyes to Henri's frowning ones.

"I'll say you have." Blanchette's voice was high and scornful. She wormed her way to the front of the

crowd, eyeing Lucie's fine new clothes pointedly. "Well. We don't include that service in this

establishment." The crowd snickered at Blanchette's coarse remark.

Tears stung Lucie's eyes as she dropped to her knees. She gathered her sodden packages and stuffed

them haphazardly back into the basket. When she salvaged what she could, she turned to leave.

Thud. Something hit the back of the head. Lucie raised her hand, a slimy substance dripping down

the back of her neck.

"You missed one of your eggs." Blanchette and Liliana stood behind her, a mocking look on

Blanchette's pretty face. Liliana silence told Lucie everything she needed to know. A lump rising in

her throat, she clutched her basket to her chest and left the tavern, letting the door swing shut

behind her.

Katherine held Lucie close, comforting her sister. "We'll leave soon – tomorrow if Father arrives.

You'll never see Annecy again." She rocked the sobbing girl in her arms. "We'll do what you said.

Start fresh. Put this all behind us."

"I know," Lucie sniffed. "But those people were my friends. Liliana was like another sister to me. And

to you. I don't understand how they could do this to us."

"They're afraid," Katherine answered. "Ever since Father lost the caravans, things haven't been the

same for anyone. When the wolves came, it made everything worse: it terrifies the Annecians, that's

not your fault. They need someone to blame it all on." Katherine lifted Jaspar, who had been

winding around her ankles, and stroked his soft fur.

"Come on, let's go to bed. Father will be home in the morning. We can decide which village to settle

in. The sea might be nice," Katherine told her sister.

Katherine helped Lucie clean the worst of the egg off her skirt before helping her get ready for bed.

Shouting dragged Lucie from a sound sleep. She leapt up from her the tiny loft bed and rushed to the

window, peering into the clearing below. A mob of villagers waving makeshift torches surrounded

the small cabin.

"Burn them, they're mages, I saw what they do!" a familiar voice shouted. It was Gus, the

shoemaker, waving a shovel over his head.

Lucie scrambled back. Horror and fear flooding her. "Katherine, they've come after me. We have to

get out of here."

The girls rushed down the narrow steps, shaking Marion awake and hurrying her toward the back

window. Just as Lucie fumbled with the latch, a rough boot splintered through the rickety front door.

Crash. The hole widened, the assault continued.

"Hurry! Hurry!" Lucie told her sisters as she crawled through the window. Katherine lifted the dazed

Marion and helped her climb through.

"Ouch." Marion tumbled through the window, landing on a patch of withered beanstalks. Katherine

dropped out behind her. The girls dashed frantically toward the back of the garden. The shadows of

the trees offered refuge. No one would dare follow them into the forest.

"You're not getting away that easy."' A dirty hand snaked out, grabbing Lucie around the waist,

yanking her off her feet. Katherine clutched Marion's hand, pulling her into the safety of the

shadows. But the mob dragged Lucie into the torchlight. She cried out in pain as they threw her to

the ground.

"You thought you'd waltz back into town after what you tried to do?" Andre, a trader who long fancied himself the town vigilante, growled. "You're no good, all of you! I lost a lot of money thanks

to your father, and now you're going to pay."

Lucie cowered as his heavy boot struck her in the side and squeezed her eyes shut against the

threatening faces crowding around her in the flickering light. After another jolt, he hoisted her to her

feet. They tightened rough ropes around her wrists before Andre dragged her struggling form

toward the wooden gate. Behind her, the men had set fire to the tiny cabin. The dry wood caught

like tinder, blazing fierce against the night sky. A tear tricked down Lucie's face.

A terrifying roar split the air. The pressure released and Andre fell back in shock and terror at the

sight appearing before him.

"Red?" Lucie cried, sobbing in relief.

Red roared louder, his unnatural form a giant silhouette against the blazing fire. Andre dropped his

torch and fled, leaving Lucie to skitter away from the spitting flames.

"How dare you?!?" Red bellowed as the men scattered. He snarled at one who had plucked up

enough bravery to wave his torch in Red's face. The man's face turned white with fear as he raced to

join his companions.

Red bellowed once more at the retreating forms, then turned to Lucie. Clumsy hands worked the

rope, growling at the red marks on her wrists. He examined her face carefully, a gentle hand tilting her chin against the light of the blaze.

"We have to go. The cowards will soon realize I'm outnumbered," Red threw the rope into the fire.

"My sisters. They're hiding in the forest." Lucie flinched as feeling flooded into her hands.

"Of course," Red rumbled. He swept Lucie in his arms and left the clearing behind.

The beast found and calmed the spooked Blackie and settled Marion on his back. Jasper had

scampered into the woods after them, and Katherine insisted on carrying him snuggled under her

chin in a makeshift sling. Leaving the blackening cabin behind them, the bedraggled group travelled

east, into the deep forest.

CHAPTER THIRTEEN

Frightened.
Lost.

Sick with grief.

The bedraggled group wandered in darkness for hours. Pushing through thick underbrush, trudging around trees, and stumbling over roots. Marion slumped over the saddle on Blackie's back, head bobbing as he ambled along. Lucie's eyes drooped with exhaustion, body and soul aching. Even Red, determinedly forging the path ahead, was flagging.

"There's an old hunting lodge nearby," Red said.

They had arrived at a rambling brook and stopped to rest. Lucie nodded, relief etching her face as

she touched a tender scratch on her cheek. Bruises bloomed where she had hit the ground. Her

entire body ached from the rough treatment it had endured.

Red eyed Lucie's wounded face and wrists, grimacing.

"You girls can rest and get cleaned up there. We'll find Pierre before we continue to the chateau," he

said.

Lucie bit her lip. What must her father be thinking? Coming home to a burnt shell of a cabin? His

daughters gone?

After a brief rest, Red urged them up, and they plodded on, until finally, when Lucie was sure she

would drop with weariness, they arrived in a small clearing. A ramshackle lodge stood tucked

beneath a cluster of towering firs, tiny against the surrounding trees. Early morning light peeked

through thick foliage, casting a pink glow across the scene.

Red opened the creaky door revealing a single room, long abandoned. A thick layer of dust covered

every surface. Only pausing to water Blackie at the nearby brook, the girls then tumbled into the

lumpy bed. Red curled up on the floor by the fireplace and they all fell asleep.

Lucie awoke and stretched, every muscle screaming in protest. Easing away from her still sleeping

sisters, she scanned the room. There wasn't much in the lodge, just a large iron pot hanging over the

fireplace, chipped plates and cups lined neatly on the dusty mantle and a dented metal bucket in the

corner. Red had disappeared, the only sign of his presence an imprint by the fireplace.

Tiptoeing across the room, Lucie gently lifted the dented bucket and stepped outside. She squinted

as bright daylight assaulted her eyes with its brilliance. Lucie picked her way down the path leading

to the brook where Blackie, happily tearing up mouthfuls of grass, whickered in greeting. After

splashing cold water on her grimy face and arms and taking a long satisfying drink, Lucie filled the

bucket and headed back to the cabin. Outside, at a wooden bench, she found Red, who had snared
two rabbits.

"We don't have any food, so they'll have to be our breakfast," Red explained. "I found some
mushrooms too, and these. They're edible." He gestured toward a limp pile of ferns.

Happy to have a plan, Lucie lit a fire with the flint left on the wooden mantle and boiled water in the
iron pot. Soon they were sitting down to a makeshift breakfast.

"Where are we?" Katherine shot Red a skittish look before reaching for another mushroom. Her
sisters were trying to exchange pleasantries, but it was obvious Red terrified them.

"A few hours north of Havre," Red answered politely, ignoring Katherine's nervousness.

"What should we do about Father?" Marion picked at the roasted meat, worry lurking in her eyes.

"Katherine, you'll stay here with Red and Marion. I'll bring Father back," Lucie decided, voice firm.

"You can't go," Katherine argued, tearing a piece of meat for Jasper. "You'll get lost."

"She's right," Marion agreed.

Annoyed, Lucie pressed her lips together tightly. It was true; Lucie's sense of direction was terrible,
and they had wandered the dark forest for miles. Left to her own devices, Lucie would never find
Annecy.

"Lucie, you stay with your sisters. I'll go." Red said, casting a protective glance at Lucie.

"But I'll have to convince Father to come with you, that we're safe," replied Lucie stubbornly.

"There's no way he'd go anywhere with you. Ever."

Red hesitated, then reluctantly nodded his shaggy head. "Only if you follow my instructions exactly; I

don't want you in any danger."

"Of course," Lucie agreed. She hovered over the mysterious greens that Red had foraged. Finally

choosing one, a bitter taste filled her mouth when she bit into it. Lucie gagged, swigging some water.

"Ugh! Those are terrible," Lucie said.

Katherine and Marion gasped in shock, waiting for repercussions from Red. He merely laughed,

refilling Lucie's cup.

"Maybe take a smaller dose next time? So greedy." He grinned at her grimacing expression.

After this, Katherine and Marion relaxed, joining in Lucie and Red's banter. Marion even

complimented Red on his roast rabbit, asking him what herbs and seasonings he had used.

After the meagre meal, Lucie and Red set off into the forest, with Katherine and Marion watching

them from the safety of the lodge. They opted to leave Blackie behind. The long journey had

exhausted Blackie, and Red said the horse's presence would give them away.

CHAPTER FOURTEEN

"We'll bring Pierre back to the chateau. There's plenty of space there. You can all stay at the chateau until you plan your move," Red instructed, leaving no room for argument.

Without Katherine and Marion holding them back, they travelled swiftly through the forest, following the brook toward Annecy.

"All right," Lucie said, ducking under a low branch. "But first we need to reach Annecy, then find Father. I wonder where he would have gone first?"

"If Pierre returned to find the cabin destroyed, he's probably gone into Annecy to find out what has happened to you girls. Do you think he'll be safe there?"

Lucie wrinkled her brow in concern, "I hope the townspeople don't attack him."

"They'd likely put him in a cell, keep him a few nights until they cool off. Where's the cell in Annecy?"

"At the hall. I think they use it for storage," Lucie replied.

"We'll look there first, then decide from there," Red said, stepping over an enormous boulder as if it were nothing. "Is there anyone you can trust in Annecy? We may need aid."

"Althea the healer will help. I've known her forever, and even when Father's business collapsed, she

was on our side." Lucie scrambled over the boulder on her hands and knees, leaving a large streak of

dirt across her cloak.

"Good. If things go wrong, we'll need her assistance," he said.

"I meant to ask," Lucie said, as she swiped a stand of hair from her cheek while avoiding a twisted

root. "How did you get to Annecy? Break the boundaries of the chateau property? Is the spell

weakening?"

"I'm not even sure myself." Red slashed his eyebrows together, thinking. "I watched the mirror, to

make sure you were safe. I saw how people in Annecy reacted to you — especially that girl."

"Blanchette." Lucie screwed up her face in in displeasure.

"Is she the blonde one?" he said.

Lucie nodded, eyes tight.

"She saw Blackie ride into Annecy. When I saw her face, I knew immediately she was a

troublemaker. So angry, so jealous. From that moment, things went downhill. She went to everyone

in town, whispering, gossiping – things were bound to boil over," Red said, finishing his sentence

with a low growl.

"But how did you leave boundary of the chateau?" Lucie turned to face Red, her eyes luminous in

the dim forest light.

"When I saw that man attack you," Red continued fiercely. "I've never been so furious, so helpless in

my entire life..." His voice trailed off. Red shook his head, clearing his thoughts. "I left the mirror, and

ran to the border where I left you. I was so frustrated. I paced back and forth, wishing I could get out

to help. Do something. And then..."

"Then what?" Lucie hopped over a patch of damp leaves.

"I just ran straight at the barrier. Closed my eyes tight and used every bit of force I possessed. I had

done this before, many times, but this time was different. There was tingling ... stinging everywhere.

And that was it. I broke the barrier."

Lucie chewed her lip. "The same magic I encountered when I touched the mirror. Did it fade?" she

said.

"It took a while to recover. My skin burned like fire. I feared crossing back to the chateau for my

horse. I might not pass the boundary a second time, so I travelled on foot. I'm fast and have an

excellent sense of direction now with the curse." Red waved a giant hand at his hairy face.

"I flew straight to Annecy to find you and your sisters. I was furious when I saw the townspeople

attacking you; I never stopped to think. I thought Lavonians were better than that." Red shook his

head in disgust, pulling a leafy branch aside for Lucie to pass.

Eventually the trees thinned and patches of sunlight appeared from the shadows of the thick green leaves. They had reached the clearing. Wisps of smoke still rose from the ashes of the old cabin.

Lucie coughed when the burning stench filled her nostrils. She picked her way through muddy boot prints, crushed grass, and the tattered remains of her precious garden.

Closer to the wreckage, Lucie's hopes of retrieving remnants of her former life were dashed. Anger blended with worry for her father, twisting in her gut. Betrayed by the people she had known and trusted all her life, Lucie choked back a sob. Red laid a comforting hand on Lucie's shoulder as she wept, turning away from her the jagged ruin of her former home.

They waited in the shadows of the trees until nightfall. When the red sky turned black, Lucie and Red trod silently down the path to the village. This time they avoided the main street, sneaking over the fence and slithering through Izzie's vegetable garden.

Judging by the raucous laughter drifting through the tavern windows, The Orc's Head was lively.

Lucie held her breath as they slunk under the kitchen window, hoping Bale, the zealous dog Henri kept to guard his chickens, wouldn't notice them. Fortunately, Bale remembered Lucie. After sniffing her hand, he swiped her cheek approvingly, returning to his kennel.

Lucie turned to Red, putting her finger to her lips as she gestured to a low building squatting in the middle of market square.

"The cell is behind that hall. That's our best chance of finding Father," she said. Her heart stumbled

in her chest as she wondered how they would free him.

Clinging to the shadows edging the buildings, Lucie led Red to the back of the town hall. Approaching

a series of square, barred windows on the ground floor, she raised herself on her tiptoes, peering

inside.

"There he is!" Lucie pointed excitedly to a crumpled form huddled on the flagstones. "I don't know

how we'll get him out though. These bars are thick." Lucie stepped aside, letting Red examine the

window.

Red prodded experimentally at the gaps between the bars. "The bars are strong," he noted, "but the

frame is weak. With leverage, I could pry the entire frame out. See, they attached the bars to the

frame, not the wall."

Red gave a snort of derision as he shook the bars, rattling the window against the frame. He scanned

the square, empty except for a few abandoned market stalls. "I need something to shove against it."

"Henri keeps a shovel in the stable — and I know where he hides the key. Would that work?" Lucie

asked.

"Too risky with the tavern that busy tonight. What about that shoemaker? He's got a shed. Would

they have one?" he gestured at the shuttered windows of the cobblers.

"Let me see, I'll be right back." Lucie darted off, returning triumphantly a few minutes later with an

iron shovel.

"Perfect," Red smiled, hefting the shovel.

"Psst! Father!" Lucie whispered, trying to get Pierre's attention. The figure on the floor stirred,

groaning and mumbling.

"Father!" Lucie hissed louder, hoping the townspeople hadn't posted guards.

"Lucie? Is it you?" Lucie's father struggled to his feet. He was slow and stiff, sporting a black eye and

a cut on his left ear.

"Shhh. We can't make much noise," Lucie warned. "We're here — Red and I — to get you out."

Lucie stood back, watching for intruders, as Red forced the shovel against the edge of the window

frame. "It will take longer because I'm trying to be quiet," Red panted, his huge bulk straining as he

shoved against the window frame. "If I can loosen it, it should pop right out."

Lucie bounced nervously on her toes as the entire base of the window screeched and splintered. Red

gave the shovel a mighty thrust, as the window-frame screamed in protest, grating as it separated

from the wooden walls. Red set the shovel down, grabbing the bars, tearing them out with a quick

tug. The entire window ripped out of the wall, leaving a yawning black hole. Red flung the window to

one side.

"Quick! Before anyone finds us," Red puffed as Lucie reached in to help her father climb over the

wreckage.

Leaving the broken window and shovel scattered on the ground, the trio crept down the lane to

Althea's cottage. "When we get there, I'll stay back," offered Red. "She'll be frightened if she sees

me like this."

"Not Althea," answered Lucie, pulling him to her side. A dim glow behind a curtain told them Althea

was still awake. Lucie knocked softly on the cottage door.

"Come in," Althea said.

She opened the door and ushered the trio inside, showing no hesitation at Red's surprising features.

She hurried them out of the cold, pouring giant mugs of fragrant tea. She also produced a plate of

buttered bread, which the grateful trio devoured. The last thing Lucie ate had been the limp carrots

and turnip scrounged from the ruins of her ravaged garden.

"We must stop meeting like this," Althea frowned as she pulled up an extra chair and gingerly

lowered herself into it, setting her cane to one side. "Tell me what brings you here this late at night. I

imagine it isn't good news."

"Lucie said you might help us." Red leaned forward across the table.

"Yes. I'll always help Lucie," Althea said. She met his gaze evenly, unafraid.

"We need supplies. We can pay you, but not right now. Those people destroyed everything in the fire." Red's voice was grim. "Food, Marion's tincture, and a waterskin is what we need."

"Of course," Althea said. She hobbled to her feet, rummaging through a cupboard in the back

bedroom. She produced a canvas rucksack and filled it with food, a blanket and, best of all, Marion's

tincture.

"Thank you, Althea." Lucie clutched the rucksack gratefully, eyes brimming with grateful tears.

"You're welcome. And especially you, my Lord." Althea turned toward Red, a knowing glint in her

eye. Althea embraced Lucie in her thin arms, surrounding her with the familiar scent of herbs and

spices. "Goodbye, dear girl, and safe journey. I'll see you again soon. I'm sure of it."

After washing down another mug of tea and taking the loaf of bread Althea had wrapped for them,

they followed Althea to the back door of her cottage. There, they slipped into the moonlit depths of

the great oak forest.

CHAPTER FIFTEEN

Tired. Numb. Exhausted.

Lucie put one foot in front of the other, trudging on through the green light filtering between the

forest leaves.

"We'll camp here." The words filtered through Lucie's thoughts. Her brain took a moment to

comprehend the meaning of the words.

Since leaving Althea's cottage, they had only stopped briefly at the lodge. Sharing some of Althea's

food with her sisters, they loaded Marion onto Blackie's back and were off. The rest of the afternoon

they walked, step by step, through the endless forest.

The anticipation of a blazing fire helped Lucie push aside her exhaustion to gather sticks. Leaving her

sisters, she ventured further into the trees. It was here that she found it. Snagged on the knobbly

branch of a scrubby pine tree, so small, so insignificant. If Lucie hadn't stooped to duck under the

branch, she would have missed it completely. A tiny scrap of cloth, ragged weather-beaten, clinging

to the rough texture of the bark. Lucie almost ignored it, but something jolted her, froze her in her

tracks.

This isn't just any cloth, Lucie peered closer, squinting. The distinctive checked pattern Father's

caravan drivers wore stared back at her. Lucie removed the faded remnant of material, careful not

to damage the fibres on the branches. Her mind raced with possibilities. How and why would her

father's caravans be this deep in the forest? Not wanting to frighten her sisters, Lucy tucked the

cloth in her pocket and went in search of Red.

"Red?"' Lucie found him gathering larger branches for the fire. Hearing the panic in Lucie's voice,

Red dropped the branches loping over to where Lucie clutched the frayed scrap tight in her hand.

"What is it?" Red ran worried eyes over her, checking for injuries.

"This." She waved the piece of fabric in her hand. Seeing his puzzled look, she explained further. "It's

the same cloth Father's caravaners wore. I found it caught on a fire tree."

Red cocked his head.

"Don't you understand? The caravans must have passed this spot," Lucie's voice rose with

excitement.

Red took the checked material in his large hand, holding it against the light and turning it back and

forth. He held it to his nose, sniffing it. "It hasn't been here long either. A few days at the most."

"Can we find out what direction they were travelling?" Lucie scanned the nearby trees, searching for

more clues.

"Show me where you found this," he told her.

Lucie led Red to the fir tree where she had found the material. Red examined the area, probing the

leaves and debris to hunt for evidence.

"Here!" Red pointed to a broken branch. "It looks like they may have gone this direction. East."

"Do you think they're close?" Lucie lowered her voice.

"It's hard to tell. Look, we'll keep this to ourselves for now. We'll light the fire, then we'll come back

and see what else we find. We don't want to give your father false hope or frighten your sisters,"

Red said. "If we find anything more substantial, we'll share it then." Red cast a cautious glance at

Lucie's sister and father.

After a meal of the bread and cheese Althea had provided, Lucie and Red slipped away, using the

pretext of foraging for mushrooms.

"I see nothing, and it's getting dark." Lucie scowled at the deepening shadows.

"We have to be patient; these things take time." Red searched through a damp patch of pine

needles. "Look over here, see this?"

Lucie leaned in close, staring at the disturbed patch of pine needles so close the spicy scent of damp

earth and moss filled her nostrils. "Do you mean those pine needles?" She pointed at the pile. "I

don't see anything." She squinted, tipped her head to see better.

"A footprint," Red explained, pointing to another disturbed patch on the forest floor. "I think they went this direction. And look here." He pointed to a birch tree. "Someone or something rubbed

against this branch. The bark is torn, something sharp — metal probably. We'll have to be on guard

and stay quiet tomorrow. Whoever took the caravans is dangerous and probably has a plan. When

we get your family safely to the chateau, I'll come back with horses, much faster and more efficient."

"I'm coming too," Lucie said stubbornly. She crossed her arms.

''There's no point arguing with you, is there?' Red asked, sighing as the pair trekked back toward the

campsite.

"Nope," Lucie grinned as she flicked back a low-hanging branch.

Red merely shook his head. "Yes, you can join me, but only if you do everything I say. These people,

whoever they are, are extremely dangerous. We're just go-ing to watch, learn what they're doing and

track them, nothing more." Red lowered his voice, giving Lucie a warning glance as the makeshift

campsite came into sight.

"Did you find mushrooms?" Katherine asked hopefully as Lucie arranged herself in a cross-legged

position next to the fire. She held her hands over the danc-ing flames, warming them.

"I didn't see any," Lucie said quickly. She looked away and busied herself brushing stray pine needles

from her dress. She hated lying — especially to her sisters.

Katherine looked suspiciously at her sister but didn't argue. She tucked Jasper into her side a bit

tighter, causing the usually docile cat to yowl in protest.

Early the next morning, they set off. Lucie and Red quietly searched for traces of the lost caravan

along the way. A few times, Lucie thought she saw another clue out of the corner of her eye, but it

was nothing. A dropped feather, an abandoned deer trail, a badger den musty with disuse. Finally,

she gave up, simply content to plod next to Blackie.

When they finally approached the chateau, the afternoon sun-streaked gold, slanting through the

towering branches of the ancient oak trees. The ragged party was hungry, dirty and spent. Lucie

sighed in relief when she saw the iron gates rising before her. She was looking forward to a hot bath

and a delicious meal.

Intimidated, Katherine and Marion hung back as Lucie strode confidently up the steps to the front

door.

"Come on," she said, beckoning her father and sisters to stand beside her as she rapped loudly with

the brass knocker.

CHAPTER SIXTEEN

Acutely aware of their dishevelled state, the sisters reluctantly trailed behind Lucie and Red up the
steps to the entrance hall. Katherine gazed in awe at the fine furnishings and polished marble floors.

"I'll get Fleur to give you staterooms near mine," Lucie chattered as she crossed the hall, gesturing
for the others to follow. "Fleur? We're back, and we have guests."

A gust of lavender-scented air breezed through the musty hall. "How delightful!" Fleur greeted the
newcomers with her tinkling old-fashioned accent. "Did I hear you say they would be staying near
your room, mistress?"

Fleur had never called Lucie mistress before. Taken aback at the title, Lucie hesitated. "Yes, can you
put them near my stateroom, Fleur? And bring tea and the strawberry tarts if there's any in the
kitchen."

"Certainly, mistress." The breeze rustled away, teasing at the ragtag group to follow.

Eyes like saucers, the sisters followed Lucie, where Fleur ensconced them in Lucie's pleasant stateroom. Lucie's father opted to take tea in his own room, insisting he needed a rest, and Red

went off on his own. Lucie suspected it was an excuse to go practice the swords.

"Would you like me to pour the tea, mistress?" asked Fleur as Katherine sat in a jacquard chair,

stroking the pattern of intricately woven fabric. Marion lay on the bed. Lucie covered her with a soft

wool blanket, propping a few pillows at her back.

The girls managed to hide their discomfort at the bizarre sight of a floating teapot pouring golden

liquid into the delicate gold-rimmed cups. After serving the strawberry tarts, Fleur wafted away. The

curtains swayed in her wake.

"This place is tenfold more astonishing that you described," Marion said. She savoured a tiny bite of

her raspberry tart, closing her eyes in bliss. "And Fleur calls you Mistress?"

"Yes," Lucie admitted, squirming a little. "That's new. She told me once she always wanted to be a

lady's maid. I guess I'm the next best thing."

Marion raised her eyebrows, glancing at Lucie over the rim of her teacup. "Well, she's very lovely."

"You can ask for whatever you want too," Lucie said before she finished her tart and picked up a tiny

sandwich. "Maribel makes the most amazing pies. And I cannot wait to show you the gardens.

They're fantastic too. When you're feeling up to it, we can go for a walk. Fleur will bring you something to wear." Lucie's trailed off as she realized she was babbling.

Marion yawned, covering her mouth delicately. "This is all so wonderful, but I'm so sleepy. I can't

even think about dinner tonight. I'm going to tuck in early; I'll see everything in the morning." She

stood up. "I'll be in my room if you need me."

Lucie watched the door close firmly behind Marion's retreating figure. "Is she all right?"

"She's having a hard time not seeing you as the little one anymore. She was like your mother, and

now you're doing everything for yourself," Katherine answered. Then, seeing Lucie's sad expression,

added quickly: "Come on, let me see these dresses you keep telling me about."

"Here, let me help you." Katherine fastened the clasp of Lucie's necklace deftly around her neck and

stepped back, examining her handiwork.

Enthralled by the fine fabrics of Lucie's dresses, she insisted on dressing them both for dinner. Her

choices were far more elaborate than Lucie would have preferred. But dresses made Katherine

happy — and that was something Lucie couldn't refuse. Even Jaspar had received a luxurious

addition, a satin collar that Katherine, with the help of Fleur, fashioned from a length of

embroidered ribbon.

"There. Beautiful." A smiled played around Katherine's lips as she stepped back to admire her

handiwork. "That cream colour suits your dark hair."

For her own dress, Katherine chose an airy concoction of pale blue lace and a gauzy cream for Lucie.

"We don't even know how to weave this pattern anymore." She touched the delicate design in the

fabric. "And this shine is divine."

"I know the necklace is extravagant, but it was a present, I think it makes him happy when I wear it,"

Lucie said. She ran her finger down the fragile chain around her neck.

"It's beautiful. What is the stone?" Katherine said, examining the green stone hanging from the

chain.

"I'm not sure," Lucie replied. The stone was the size of her thumb; a clear, brilliant green. "He says

his mother has a similar one."

A tiny wrinkle appeared between Katherine's eyes. "Are you sure it's wise to take a gift like that from

Red?"

Lucie shrugged, uncomfortable under the scrutiny of her sister. "It seemed rude to refuse." She

averted her eyes.

Katherine looked critically at her sash, making a tiny adjustment. "Well, I certainly can see he thinks

the world of you."

"I know," Lucie sighed as she picked up a hairbrush, then set it down again. "I just wish I could help

him break that curse."

Katherine placed a comforting hand on her sister's back. "You will find a way. I know it. Now let's collect Father and go to dinner. I hope we're having one of these wonderful pies you keep telling me about." Katherine linked arms with her sister.

CHAPTER SEVENTEEN

Daybreak pierced the sky with narrow bands of pink and orange as Lucie and Red left the chateau

boundaries early the next morning. This time, they were well prepared with two horses loaded with

supplies to last at least a week. Nerves fluttered in Lucie's chest as they approached the verge of the

great oak forest.

"Do you think you can cross the barrier again?" Lucie worried. She grasped the strap of her reins and

turned in her saddle toward Red.

"We'll have to try. If you lead the horses across, I'll run toward you. That's what broke the boundary

before. I focused on moving toward something ... someone."

Lucie dismounted, leading Blackie and Lantic, Red's charger, toward a stand of fir. A familiar buzzing

hummed in the air along with that strange tingling sensation. Magic washed over her skin as Lucie

passed under the soaring branches of the last oak tree.

"I felt something there," she said. She pointed to the great oak. "If you get past the oak, you'll cross

the boundary."

Red gritted his teeth and took a running start, his eyes fierce as he charged toward Lucie. Loud

crackling and fizzing split the air as Red approached the barrier. Closing his eyes tight, he threw

himself forward with a bellow. Sparks flew from his skin as he crashed through the barrier and

tumbled to the ground, coughing and gasping for breath.

"You did it," Lucie said. She knelt beside him, putting a hand to his arm. It still sizzled faintly with

magic. Red opened his eyes slowly, heaving as he recovered his breath.

"How do you feel?" Lucie's worried eyes met his.

"Never better," Red grinned, pushing to his feet. And they were off. The sun slid high in the deep

blue. The forest surrounded them with the twittering of birds, the chattering brook, and the wind

rustling through the leaves.

"How much farther?" Lucie chewed one of Maribel's delicious savoury pies. After an uneventful ride,

they stopped to lunch near a small brook that rippled under the shadows of a large fir tree. The

horses drank deeply from its clear water, shaking showers of droplets into crisp pine scented air.

"Two hours if we keep up this pace," Red said, lounging against a giant tree root. "It's much faster

with horses."

Lucie licked the last crumbs from her fingers. "What happens when we find the caravans?" She

rummaged through the pack for her flask, taking a sip of the lemonade Maribel sent.

"Whoever is responsible clearly outnumbers us. And they have a plan. The smartest move we can

make is get a location, learn who's behind them and what they're planning. Then report directly to

King Erich. I have a message for him anyway." Red pressed his lips together, a determined light

gleaming from darkening eyes.

"Waltz into the palace and ask to speak to the King?" Lucie choked, spitting lemonade. Approaching

King Erich directly would never in a thousand years have occurred to Lucie.

"I'll take care of that," Red replied. He thumped Lucie on the back until she recovered her breath.

"We just need to gather intelligence. I mean, I know something is in that forest. But we need solid

information to present to the King's council before King Erich can decide about the bandits.

Suspicions won't work."

Lucie stood up, brushing off her riding clothes. "Let's not waste time then," she said. She gathered

the scattered remains of their lunch, stuffing them into a saddlebag.

"We're close," Red said.

A few hours of steady riding combined with Red's uncanny sense of direction brought them back to

the small clearing where Lucie had found the scrap of cloth. Slowly, surely, Red followed the trail,

uncovering a track that eventually widened into a path through thick trees and underbrush.

"Wait." Red held up a hand, signalling for Lucie to pause. "I see something. Look over there."

Lucie followed Red's pointing finger. Her breath caught in dismay at the sight. Horror. Grief. Dread.

At the bottom of a narrow ravine lay the scattered remains of twisted wreckage. The missing caravans.

"What happened?" Lucie knelt in the sooty debris, picking up the tarnished remains of what once was a fine silver bowl. She had seen similar; Father routinely ordered them from his eastern trade route.

"I think they attacked from that direction." Red pointed toward a break in the trees. "They probably waited in a sheltered area beside the trail, then forced through the trees, took what they could and burned the rest." His eyes rested on a charred wagon wheel; spokes reduced to jagged shards pointing at the sky.

"Where do you think the people are? Father's caravan traders?" Lucie asked, afraid to even think of the appalling possibilities. "There aren't any bodies, are there?" she searched the debris with uneasy eyes.

"We won't know until we search," Red answered, a grim expression crossing his face.

He headed toward an overturned caravan, still half intact; it's open door yawning with gruesome possibilities. The pair spent a few tense minutes examining the site, but Lucie saw it first. Half buried in the ground and burned beyond recognition; they could only assume it was one of the bodies of

Father's caravaners. After a thorough search, they found five bodies.

"Is this everyone?" asked Red after exhausting every nook and cranny of the site.

"This caravan group had seven traders. We're still missing two people. Do you think they're alive?"

Lucie sank onto a damp pile of leaves, dropping her head in her hands. A streak of soot covered her

face; grit lined her fingernails. The stench of ashes and decay hung thick in the air – air heavy and

sour with sorrow.

Red rested next to her, his face grim. "I hope so. The only thing we can do is give them a proper

burial. Pay our respects," he said.

It was a long dirty job that brought them well into evening. When they finished, Lucie made simple

wooden markers from salvaged scraps, placing them gently. They stood at the mound. Silent.

Somber in the twilight.

"Let them never be forgotten," Lucie whispered, before turning to go. Red followed close behind.

Subdued, the two trudged back to the waiting horses, making camp at the brook. Lucie didn't want

to be in sight of their grim findings, and neither did Red. The next morning, they left the horses at

camp before making a final reluctant return to the wreckage.

"I suspect the bandits travelled this direction. They were so deep in the forest; they didn't think even

attempt to hide their tracks." Red pointed to a cluster of muddled footprints leading down the

ravine. "And it appears like there's a good-sized group."

"Let's go find them," Lucie said. She set her chin steadily, following Red, who led the way down the

narrow track.

"I hear something!" Lucie froze, holding her finger to her lips as she strained her ears.

In the distance rang the sound of a pounding mallet. Faint, but unmistakable. With Red leading, they

crept, pushing through thick underbrush. Slowly. Carefully. As they drew closer, Lucie heard more

voices and tools being used — even the distinct thump of clothes washed against a rock in the

stream.

They slithered behind a large tree, peering out. Before them lay a large, well-established camp

housing at least fifty people. Lucie watched, wide-eyed, at the hive of activity. Two men stirred a pot

that bubbled over a fire, others stacked firewood, and two women did the washing.

"An army camp," whispered Red. "Look! That's where they store weapons."

He used his chin to point toward a square canvas tent. Stacks of weapons stuck out through the door

flap – knives, swords, spears, and sheaves of arrows.

"Who are these people? They're surely not ordinary bandits," Lucie said, pressing herself flat against the tree.

"They're not Lavonian soldiers," answered Red. "They're from Iasia. Look at the crest on the tunics. I

knew things were tense, but I didn't know they were this serious." His expert eyes scanned the

encampment, searching for information. "Look, guards on duty as well. Doing rounds."

He pulled Lucie under the safety of some underbrush as a man swinging an enormous sword and

whistling strolled their way. They watched from the shadows as he passed by, oblivious to their

presence.

"They might be well guarded," Red said once they crept a safe distance away from the bandit camp.

"But they're careless. Complacent."

"But why?"

Evening had fallen, Lucie and Red were sitting by the fire, Lucie poked a stick at the glowing coals. "I

thought things were peaceful between Lovan and Iasia."

"Penelope." Red tasted the pot of stew he was making for dinner. The scent of the spice and herbs

he added made Lucie's stomach growl. "She's causing trouble. I guess she figured the best way to

weaken Lovan is to destroy trade relations. Judging from that bandit camp, Penelope has been

developing this plan for a while. She probably used soldiers to pose as traders and infiltrate the

caravans. She knows Lovan depends on trade and especially depends on this route from Iasia. That's why the alliance was so important for Lovan." Red tossed another log on the fire, sending showers of

sparks shooting into the air.

"But the Alliance fell apart when Prince Frederich disappeared. What does Penelope think she'll gain

by destroying our trade?" she said.

Glowing embers cast a rosy glow across Lucie's face. "Doesn't the benefit go both ways? Doesn't

Iasia need to go through Lovan to trade with Luixe and don't the Iasians need trade with Lovan

themselves?"

"Iaisa can trade with Luixe directly now. They expanded their navy and rebuilt the harbour," he said.

explained Red, scooping the savoury stew into two bowls. "It's quicker for the Iasians to trade by sea

too." He leaned back against his bedroll, blowing on the spicy stew. "Penelope's had the Iasians

digging out the Florin harbour for years, building taverns and inns for merchant fleets. We'll have to

get word to King Erich immediately." Red took a bite of steaming hot stew.

"Us?" Lucie squeaked. A myriad of feelings rippled through her. Excitement. Fear. Apprehension.

"You've got nothing to worry about, I'll get you into the castle. You'll be safe." said Red. "I just can't

speak to King Erich myself yet — not when I'm like—this." He pulled on a shaggy ear in frustration.

"We'll leave in the morning."

"Are you really sure about this?" Lucie still argued as they rode the dusty road toward Corvan and

King Erich's castle.

Lucie waved at a stray mosquito, adjusting her position in the saddle. It was dark. They travelled at

night now, slipping through fields, skirting around villages, camping deep in the forest at night.

The last thing Red needed was to terrorise the farmers, starting a whirlwind of wild rumours, Red

explained to Lucie as they cut through an apple orchard. It was getting harder to stay undercover

now. They were close to the city, even now. Warm light shone from a farmhouse cottage across the

orchard, faint voices drifted through the apple trees.

"We'll go through the city after sunset. I know a back entrance into the castle grounds; if it's dark,

we'll stay out of sight," explained Red, steering his horse around a cluster of slumbering sheep. "If

we're careful, I think we can stay undercover all the way through Corvan. There are cottages on the

edge of the grounds. They are only used for overflow guests at festivals, so they'll be empty. No one

goes near them the rest of the time."

"Then what?" Lucie asked, hesitation in her eyes. "What should I say?" Lucie was nervous and

apprehensive about meeting members of the royal family, or the king's guards for that matter. Why

should anyone believe Lucie, an insignificant country girl? Red, however, was supremely confident.

"If you deliver this ring," he said. Red reached in the pocket of his breeches and brought out a thick gold signet ring. "They'll take you straight to King Erich. Explain everything we saw; make sure Queen

Isabella is present, she'll be sympathetic. If we arrive around dinnertime, you can catch them

together."

The heavy gold ring was far too big for Lucie's slender fingers, so she found a piece of string and tied

it around her neck, the tug of its weight a solid reminder of her responsibility.

That evening, Red covered his giant form with a hooded cloak and led Lucie through the narrow back

streets of Corvan. A blanket of darkness provided them with an extra measure of invisibility.

Although the clatter of the horses' hooves brought curious looks, the city brought so many visitors

that they remained unnoticed. When they reached the towering stone walls of the castle, Red led

Lucie to a narrow side gate, nearly unnoticeable under a curtain of long, hanging vines.

"I know there's a key here somewhere," Red muttered, hunting under a collection of lumpy stones

piled near the gate. He lifted one after the other. "Ahh … here we go."

He produced a rusty iron key, fitted it into the lock, which turned with a screech of metal. The gate

creaked open. They were in.

Lucie's heart beat like a hammer against her chest. It seemed too easy, too simple. After scanning

the area for guards and castle staff, they led the horses through, grass muffling their hooves. The gate swung shut, the latch clicked firmly into place, and Red pocketed the key. Then, sheltering

under the trees clustering the outskirts of the grounds, they sneaked around the parameter until

they reached a series of quaint stone cottages.

"I'll stay here," Red said as he dismounted near the end cottage. It was well out of sight, set back

behind a flowering hedge. "Remember, they can't see me like this. If they insist – trust me, they will

– Queen Isabella can be very persuasive, don't give in." Red's voice was steely with determination.

Apprehension gripped Lucie as she craned her neck up at the ramparts and towers looming over her.

"What if they don't believe me?" she asked.

Red held Lucie by the shoulders, searching her eyes. "You can do this. I know you can. You're the

bravest girl I know."

Lucie took a deep breath, steadying herself, forcing the wobble out of her voice. "Right then," she

said. Leaving Red behind, she straightened her spine and set off through the garden.

CHAPTER EIGHTEEN

Lucie's bravery deserted her as she picked her way across the stone courtyard. She took a deep
breath, approached a side door and knocked. The sound echoed. Hollow. Loud.

"Hello?" Lucie called. The moments ticked by. Finally—finally—a smartly uniformed girl cracked the
door open.

"Yes?" the girl's brow crinkled, questions swimming in her eyes as she scanned Lucie's rumpled and
old-fashioned, but very rich attire. "Can I assist you, my lady?"

"Yes." Lucie ignored the title to focus on her mission. "I need to see King Erich. I have an important
message for him. It's urgent."

"He's not seeing anyone at the minute. The next audience is Tuesday. Through the main gate and to
the audience hall like other citizens," the girl said in a polite, but firm manner. She started to pull the
door shut behind her.

Lucie caught the door, wedging it open with her foot. "It's urgent," she insisted.

"Everyone has something urgent, my lady," the girl said.

Deciding Lucie wasn't as important as she first thought, the girl shoved the door impatiently, trying

to move the foot Lucie stubbornly jammed between the door and the frame.

Lucie held firm, drawing the ring from around her neck, dangling it in front of the girl. "Look, I have

this ring," Lucie said.

The heavy gold reflected the light, swinging from her fingers. The girl leaned forward, squinting at

the ring. "Wait here," she told Lucie.

Abruptly she left, leaving Lucie standing at the door. A few minutes later, the girl returned,

accompanied by a tall stern woman. The starched grey dress and scraped back hair told Lucie this

woman suffered no nonsense.

"Delphine informed me you have an urgent message for His Majesty?" the woman raised her thin

eyebrows. "I must say, this is highly unusual."

"Yes. I do." Lucie met the woman's gaze evenly.

"Can you tell me the nature of this message? Perhaps I could pass it along for you?"

"No. Just that it's urgent. Very urgent. And I have this token." Lucie again held out the ring, this time

receiving a quite different reaction.

The woman's thin face greyed, mouth gaping in astonishment at the ring. Immediately, her

demeanour softened.

"Follow me. I'll take you to King Erich myself. Delphine, see that we prepare a stateroom for

lady....?" She turned questioningly to Lucie.

"Lucie."

"For Lady Lucie. She may need to stay tonight. See that they provide her the means to … freshen

up."

"Right away Mistress Marthe," the girl replied. Wide-eyed, the girl bobbed a curtsy and darted away.

Lucie trotted behind the dour-faced woman as they wound their way through the castle.

"The family is at dinner," Marthe explained as they made their way down a stone corridor lined with

doors. "But I believe His Highness would not want this matter to wait." She halted in front of an

ornate panelled door, rapping smartly before opening it.

Lucie was suddenly very aware of her tattered and grimy appearance as she took in the scene before

her. Three richly dressed people were sitting at a large table. Delicate china, silver and crystal,

gleamed from its polished surface. Heavy silk curtains and fine paintings hung from panelled walls

and a crackling fire roared in the fireplace, lending the room a cosy glow despite its ornate

furnishings. Lucie's stomach rumbled as the smell of rich roast beef and gravy wafted towards her.

"What is it, Marthe?" King Erich's brow furrowed in concern when he saw Marthe's face. He stood

abruptly, nearly knocking over a crystal decanter in his rush.

"Your Majesty, I believe you might be interested in what this young woman, Lady Lucie, has to say."

The woman curtsied deeply, stiff material of her dress rustling with the movement. King Erich sat down.

"Have a seat, my dear," the king said. He waved at Marthe, who curtsied again before turning.

The door closed softly behind her. Lucie was alone with the royal family. Her pulse thumped, heart pounding fiercely.

"I have this to show you," Lucie said. She perched on the edge of a brocade chair, being careful not to smudge it. She pulled the ring from around her neck and handed it to King Erich, tucking her hands underneath her.

King Erich examined the ring from all angles, an expression of curiosity changing to concern as he turned the ring in his hand. Without a word, he handed it to Queen Isabel, who immediately turned pale. She seemed to hold back a gasp of dismay as she clutched the ring in her delicate hand.

"Where did you find this ring?" King Erich asked, his face grim as he turned his eyes to Lucie. Queen Isabel and Princess Celine leaned forward to hear her answer.

"A friend gave it to me," Lucie faltered. "He – he requested he remain anonymous."

"Tell us about this friend? Is he nearby? What does he look like?" King Erich gripped the edge of the table so hard his knuckles turned white.

"I wish I could tell you," Lucie hesitated, plucking at a small tear in her dress. "But he made me promise not to. I can't break my word, not even for you, Your Majesty. I'm here to pass along his

message to you; it's of utmost importance."

She slid her eyes to Queen Isabella, whose lip trembled with unspoken emotion. She suddenly

wished she could tell them everything. Queen Isabella looked so sad and yet so hopeful.

"We're listening." King Erich let out a long breath, leaning back against his chair.

King Erich's face grew more and more solemn as Lucie told the entire tale. How they discovered the

bandits, facts about how they affected the trade routes to Iaisia, ending with the Iasian betrayal.

King Erich threaded his fingers together on the table. "I'll hold an emergency meeting with my

council tomorrow, but we must keep this quiet. If people learn the Iasian Alliance is broken to this

extent and think we're under attack, they'll revolt. It will cause outright war. Not to mention the

magic issue. We'll deal with this quietly or it will cause even more unrest than Lovan already

suffers."

Lucie met King Erich's eyes. "I understand, Your Majesty."

"Will you join the council meeting tomorrow and explain everything you encountered?" Queen

Isabella's patrician voice entered the conversation.

Lucie gulped, the thought of speaking before the most important leaders in the kingdom terrified

her. "Of course," she said. She drew her shoulders back, chasing the weakness from her voice.

"And Lucie," Queen Isabella interjected, eyes soft with emotion. "Anything — anything — you can

tell us about Red, don't hesitate to share. Please." Lucie's heart broke at the pleading expression on

Isabella's face.

"Of course," Lucie answered gently, desperately wishing she could tell Queen Isabella more about

Red.

A starched maid ushered Lucie to a comfortable stateroom where she washed away the travel grime

and dressed in the impractical, but clean, gown brought for her. She wolfed down a meal of cold

chicken sandwiches washed with strong tea before deciding to find Red.

Locking the door to avoid curious eyes, Lucie pulled on her boots, then arranged pillows under the

bedclothes until they resembled a human form. Satisfied, she opened the door, quietly peeping

down the corridor, checking for observers. She tiptoed noiselessly along stone halls. By trial and

error, Lucie returned to the back door she had come through. Wadding some material in the latch to

keep it cracked open, she crept to Red's cottage on the edge of the grounds. She found Red sitting

by a small pond, staring gloomily at the lily-covered water.

Red sprung up as Lucie approached. "Did you talk to the king and queen?" he asked. Red's voice was

eager, nervous.

"Yes." Lucie plopped down on the smooth grass. "King Erich's calling the council tomorrow. He wants me to speak to them, tell them what we discovered. I showed King Erich and Queen Isabella

the ring. You were right. They were desperate to know how I received it." Lucie's voice trailed

uncertainly. "I didn't know what to say ... Queen Isabella looked so upset. Devastated."

Red shifted uncomfortably and scratched his chin with a big, furry hand. "What did you tell them?"

"I didn't know how to answer," Lucie replied, exasperation crossing her face. "I didn't tell them

where you are, if that's what you mean. I really don't have a clue who you are, not really. I don't

even know what your proper name is." Lucie plucked a blade of grass, rubbing it between her thumb

and forefinger.

Red drooped. "I'm sorry. I really am. It's just that I'm not ready to meet them — yet."

Lucie nodded. "I know. It was just uncomfortable. Princess Celine was nearly in tears."

Red lowered his enormous head, resting it on giant knees. "I wish I could do something to make this

easier."

"It's all right. I'm glad to help. Marthe assigned me a state-room in the castle. I can't stay here

though. They might come looking for me."

"The east wing?"

"I think so," Lucie frowned. "I'm not very good at directions."

"Good," Red exhaled. "Queen Isabella only puts people she likes in the east wing."

"Well, I think I like them too." Despite her nerves, Lucie was drawn to the elegant Queen Isabella

and felt that in different circumstances, she and the perky golden-haired Princess Celine would have

become friends.

"Just do one thing. It is of utmost importance," Red continued, a tiny smirk lightening the sober

expression on his face.

"What?" Lucie jerked her head up suspiciously.

"Take the twig out of your hair before you meet the king's council tomorrow."

Lucie reached up, pulling the offending stick from her hair. "Why didn't you tell me earlier?" she

laughed, tossing the twig at the teasing Red, who dodged it easily.

The next morning, Lucie donned the borrowed dress they had provided her, cinching the loose

waistband with a belt. A uniformed maid arranged her hair into stiff curls. Lucie grimaced, putting a

hand up to touch her tender scalp, missing Fleur's gentle hands.

Since Lucie only had bed slippers and travelling boots, she opted for the boots, hoping they wouldn't

show beneath the long gown. Deeming herself ready, she gathered her courage, took one last sip

from the cooling tea, and steeled her spine before being led through the endless corridors of the

Lavonian castle.

Lucie knocked softly on the heavy door before pushing it open, glancing around with timid eyes. King

Erich's council comprised the most important nobles in Lavon, and they were all presently gathered around an endless table. Lucie stood hesitantly in the doorway, wondering what to do next.

"Please, sit," King Erich said, gesturing toward an empty seat near him.

Footsteps whispering against the carpet, Lucie made her way over to a high-backed chair. She seated herself, smoothing sweaty hands on her gown. Queen Isabella leaned around King Erich to give Lucie an encouraging nod as she settled. Her cheeks reddened under the sea of curious faces. All wondering what she, a young unknown slip of a girl, was doing in King Erich's council chambers.

"We have reason to believe the Alliance with Iasia has been violated," King Erich cleared his throat, speaking solemnly. "And Lady Lucie of?" he broke off, giving Lucie a questioning look.

"Annecy," Lucie replied. "And it's not Lady Lucie, Your Majesty, just Lucie of Annecy." She squeezed her hands tightly in her lap as the nobles exchanged dubious glances.

"A commoner." Lucie flushed as she overheard a man in a red velvet jacket murmur the sentiment, she was sure many others were thinking. Lucie slid her gaze from him and braced herself against eyes boring into her as King Erich continued.

"Lucie discovered something significant that I believe is of utmost priority and urgency," the king said. King Erich threw the red jacketed noble a sharp look.

"Lucie?" King Erich gestured for her to speak.

Lucie took a deep breath and in a shaky voice explained to the council their discoveries about the Iasian bandits.

"And you say there was magic involved?" a tall thin man sitting near the king asked, face twisted with a distasteful expression.

"Yes," Lucie replied, scraping the fortitude to return his stare evenly. "Someone, from the Iasian nobility cursed one of our citizens." The bold statement caused a chorus of mutters around the table.

"Magic is strictly outlawed here in Lovan. It's against the terms of the Iasian Alliance for Iasians to practice here. That's always been our terms," the noble, expensively dressed, spit out the words, his stiffly coiffed hair trembling in indignation. The other nobles nodded in agreement. Again, a rumble of discontent circled the table.

"And you think the Iasians sank Prince Frederich's ship? Does our spymaster have an opinion regarding this?" an older man leaned forward, eyes intent.

"We can't answer that question — yet." A grave expression crossed King Erich's face. "But we can be sure the Iasians are weakening us. Destroying our trade, unsettling our citizens, even at the expense of our longstanding alliance. We cannot allow this to continue."

"This must mean war!" a giant black-haired man cried out, pounding the table. He was younger than the other nobles and much more exuberant in his opinions.

Cries of agreement met his enthusiasm along with arguments from around the table.

"Can we verify this girl tells the truth?" one of the nobles spoke up with a frown. "I mean, this girl,

Lucie? No one's even heard of her before. She came from nowhere. How do we know she's not a

troublemaker?"

A chorus of agreement rose from around the table. Lucie's faced burned hot as she squirmed in her

seat, wishing she could disappear.

"We vouch for Lucie ourselves," King Erich said. He glanced toward Queen Isabella, who nodded her

elegant head in accord.

"If this is the case — you seem convinced it is — we must move swiftly," the older man spoke again.

"If what Lucie says is true, it's clear the Iasians mean to cause serious harm. If possible, we must deal

with the bandits yet prevent outright war." He glared pointedly at the black-haired man, who

lowered his bushy eyebrows in response.

"Crin, you're saying that because your land borders Iasia, you have the most to lose if we go to

war?" the black-haired man said. He thrust a calloused hand through unruly curls.

"Yes," the older noble replied calmy. "I do have much to lose. But so do us all." His steady eyes

travelled around the table; unflinching. Several nobles looked away, uncomfortable expressions

lurking on their faces.

"Lucie," interrupted King Erich, putting a halt to the brewing argument. "Was there anything else
you needed to tell us? About the magic or the Iasian Bandits? Do you feel confident that you could
lead a contingent to their camp?"

"I believe so," Lucie wavered, hoping Red would provide help with his superior sense of direction.

"Well, in that case, thank you, Lucie, for your assistance and willingness to come forward." King Erich
dismissed Lucie. "It seems we have much to discuss. Would you be willing to remain at the castle
until we make our decision? We may need you later." King Erich waited for Lucie's answer.

"Of course," Lucie said. She stood up, legs still shaking. Truthfully, she would prefer a dozen burning
cabins and an entire army of bandits than face the scrutiny of the council again, but if needed, she
would go along with them. Lucie managed to stumble to the door without tripping. In the safety of
the corridor, she collapsed against the wall, relief washing over her. Now, to share the news with
Red.

Lucie arrived back at her stateroom hoping to hole up until dinner, but unfortunately Princess Celine
discovered her and barged in with a flurry of golden hair and dramatic hand gestures.

"They have never invited me to Father's council meeting," Celine complained. She widened her big
blue eyes and plucked a loose thread on one of the plethora of decorative pillows scattered across

the bed.

Lucie rolled her eyes. "Trust me, you're not missing much."

"I suppose," Celine sighed. "But I'm going to have to learn. Father thinks I'm such a baby." She rolled

onto her back, clutching the pillow to her chest.

Lucie crinkled her nose. "What about Frederich? Was he invited to the king's council meetings?"

Celine scoffed. "Yes, always. They involved him in everything; but Frederich and Father were always

butting heads, especially about magic. Frederick thought since he was marrying Penelope, they

should lift the ban on magic. I mean, it is behind the times. We're the only country where magic is

outlawed. That's the major subject they argued about before Frederich left. Before he-" Celine

halted abruptly. Sitting up, she flicked back her waterfall of hair.

"Really? They argued?" Lucie had always imagined a rosy picture-perfect version of life in the royal

castle. She thought it would be all ballgowns, fancy dinners and soirees, not council meetings and

arguments about politics.

"Not a lot. Frederich was pretty easy-going, and Father is fair most of the time. But this really

bothered Frederich because he had spent time outside Lovanian borders — more than most people.

Frederich saw how well magic worked for other kingdoms and he wanted Lovanians to have those

opportunities. He told me once he thinks there are people in Lovan with magic they're forced to hide

... or aren't even aware of. Many people." Although they were the only ones in the stateroom, Celine

lowered her voice, her eyes darting.

"Were you and Frederich close?" Lucie sat on the bed next to Celine.

"Yes. Frederich was wonderful, never acted like he was better than me and always invited me to join

his lessons. That's how I learned to use the sword. Frederich used to practice with me in the early

mornings ... every day unless he was away." A faraway look drifted across Celine's face.

"I miss him all the time. And there's no one to talk to about Frederich. I mean, he was going to marry

Penelope from Iasia, but I knew the girls in court hoped he would change his mind and choose one

of them instead. Obviously, he couldn't. It would break the terms of the Alliance, but it meant I

couldn't talk to them about Frederich. They would just try to pry information out of me, or use me to

get closer to him. And now I have to be queen; I still can't talk to them; They only befriend me

because they want power and position."

Lucie swung her legs up, settling into a comfortable spot on the bed. "What about your mother and

father? Do you discuss this with them? They seem understanding."

"I could — and probably should — but they miss Frederich too. It changed everything when he

disappeared. Mother used to laugh and throw parties. Now she only socialises because she has to.

Father thinks if he wraps me in cotton wool, he can keep me safe. That's why I'm never in council meetings." Celine pouted.

Lucie laid a hand on the younger girl's shoulder. "I lost someone too. You're right. It changes everything. But you need to tell them how you feel, if not for yourself, for King Erich and Queen Isobella. For Lovan. They need you involved, especially now. The alliance is on shaky ground."

Celine nodded as Lucie bit her lip, hoping she hadn't crossed too many boundaries with this girl who seemed so young and so green.

It was late afternoon when the council emerged. Exhausted, King Erich and Queen Isabella sat at the dinner table where Celine had insisted on Lucie joining them. She had even coaxed Lucie to squeeze into an exquisite, but extremely stiff, uncomfortable dress.

"It's finally decided," King Erich said. He dug his fork into fluffy mashed potatoes, a dribble of salty gravy sliding down to puddle in the roast carrots.

"What did the council decide, Father?" Celine said, then sipped daintily from a crystal goblet.

"We're not going to war, thank goodness. Gunther always wants war. He's a brilliant strategist though, I need him on the council. But we will take action by sending a message to Iasia."

King Erich took another forkful, turning to Lucie. "We'll need you to lead us to the bandit camp. We'll send a small raiding party, nothing significant enough to cause panic. You don't have to fight obviously, just show us the location."

"You will still need a weapon to protect yourself. As a precaution," King Erich continued. "Celine can

escort you to the armoury tomorrow to get kitted out."

Celine grinned over the rim of her glass, excited to be included.

Icy fingers of fear clutched at Lucie's chest. "Me?" she squeaked, nearly choking on a carrot. Lucie

had never touched a weapon, let alone used one.

"Only as a precaution, of course," Queen Isabella repeated consolingly, flashing King Erich a warning

look. "It's very unlikely you'll see fighting. Remember, the raiding party will be King Erich's best men.

You have nothing to worry about."

Lucie nibbled at her asparagus, trying not to drip butter on the very expensive dress she was

wearing. "I can do that," she said.

"If there's nothing to worry about, can I join the raiding party?" Celine interrupted, leaning her

elbows eagerly on the table.

"I think your mother needs you here, darling," King Erich said as he slid his eyes to Queen Isabella.

"I never get to do anything exciting," Celine slumped, pouting prettily.

"We'll take the horses to the beach while they are away," Queen Isabella comforted Celine. "Maybe

hold a picnic?"

Celine sulked, refusing to be consoled. "I suppose," she said.

Dinner ran long. Lucie wondered how the royal family had time for anything besides eating and

meals. It was late when Lucie finally slipped past the castle staff and snuck away to Red's cottage.

"I didn't know if they had food in the cottage, so I brought you some rolls," Lucie said. She fished in

the pocket of her gown, producing squashed sweet rolls she had swiped from her stateroom.

"Thanks!" Red said. He gobbled a roll, devouring it in a single bite. "What did the council say?"

"They only invited me for the beginning of the council meeting. There was lots of arguing." Lucie

plopped in a velvet chair and drew a fluffy blanket around her shoulder. Red hadn't lit the fire in

case anyone saw it and investigated.

"Of course," Red said. He rolled his eyes as he tore into another roll. "Was Lord Gunther there?"

"I don't know, they didn't tell me names. Which one is Lord Gunther?" Lucie turned the pocket of

the gown inside out, attempting to brush the crumbs from the fabric.

"Big, tall, lots of black hair and giant eyebrows. He wore a big beard for a while. He thought he was a

pirate."

"Oh, him," she replied. A smudge of jam clung to Lucie's finger, and she licked it off. "Lord Gunther

was in the council. He doesn't seem to get along with the older one very well."

"Lord Hugo? Did he have grey hair tied back really tight? Black spectacles?"

"Yes. He seemed the most calm and reasonable."

"He is," agreed Red. "I think he's King Erich's favourite. He'd never say it though, doesn't want to

cause too much friction. People are jealous."

"Good luck with that," Lucie huffed.

"So, what did the council decide?" Red drew the subject back to the matter at hand.

"They're sending a raiding party. A small one, King Erich said."

Red nodded. "I thought that was the best idea. I'm guessing Lord Hugo came up with that one," he

said. "They can't be obvious. That's why they need to keep the raiding party small. Make it seem like

they came across the bandits accidentally. When is the party leaving?"

"In the next few days, as soon as they prepare," Lucie said. She paused, tracing a pattern on the

ground with her foot. Now came the tricky part. Asking Red for help. Lucie swallowed and

approached the subject cautiously. "King Erich asked me to go with their raiding party to show them

where the camp is located."

Red nodded, not surprised by this announcement "I expected as much. How do you feel about

joining them, are you willing to go?"

"The only problem..." Lucie hesitated. "I don't exactly know where the bandit camp is. I'm terrible at

directions. Can you...?" her voice trailed off hopefully.

"Of course." Red chomped down on the last roll, brushing the crumbs from his hands. "I would hardly expect you to go alone."

"But won't they – you know – see you?" Concern flitted across Lucie's face.

"I'll follow them through the woods. Even the best trackers in the country can't catch me. I'll show

you where to go and leave a trail to follow."

Lucie heaved a sigh of relief, the apprehension seeping out of her.

"And another thing. King Erich wants me to carry a weapon. Me. I've never held a weapon in my life.

I'll probably cut my own hand off," Lucie said.

Red chuckled. "I'll show you some basics before you go — or Celine will. Don't worry. You won't

have to actually use it, I'll stay close, and King Erich's men won't let you near any fighting. King Erich

keeps a reserve of his best soldiers here. They'll be in and out before anyone notices."

"I hope so," she said.

The next few days flew by in a flurry of activity. Celine took Lucie to the armoury where they fitted

her with a few pieces of light armour: a small, but deadly looking sword, which terrified her to no

end, and a whip-sharp dagger that fit into a cunning leather case strapped to her boot.

"I like the dagger; it looks handy. But I'm not confident with the sword." Lucie swung the sword in an

ungainly circle around her head.

Celine's eyes sparkled, giggling at Lucie's clumsy attempt. "Do it like this," Celine said.

Celine's own sword swept the air – a blur of motion, dancing in a graceful arc that ended with her

leaping forward into a graceful pose.

"You need to take it down a notch. Can you show me something simple?" Lucie insisted as the dust

swirled and settled into a fine mist over the arena. "I can't learn all that in two days."

"Fine," Celine said, sliding her sword back into its scabbard. "First, you positioned your feet wrong.

Your need to move with your hips, like this." Celine demonstrated, then positioned Lucie's hips,

placing her feet in the correct stance. "Then you'll have more power behind you, and you'll be able

to react quicker when you need to feint or dodge."

Lucie bounced on her toes in her best attempt to imitate Celine's movements.

"There. That's ... better," Celine said, giving Lucie's pose a considering examination. "Then, you hold

the sword like this." She adjusted Lucie's grip on the sword. "That way you'll be ready for whatever

comes at you from any direction."

Lucie nodded. "Hips ready, hands ready," she said. Her boots scraped against the grit of the arena

floor as she practiced the moves.

"Yes. Then watch, think, predict what your opponent is planning before they move. That's the part

that takes practice," Celine instructed. "If we had time, I'd set up practice rounds with the

instructors, but for now I'll do it." Celine stepped back a few paces. "I'm going to come at you, try to remember what I said. Remember, they're only practice swords. Be bold."

Lucie stiffly placed her feet into the positions Celine had shown her. "Ready!" she called, her sword

sliding against the sweat on her palms.

Celine sprang forward, whipped out her practice sword and had Lucie disarmed in a swing and a deft

jab.

"I'm never going to get it," Lucie complained, rubbing her stinging arm.

"You will," Celine said. She was all business. "You don't need to know everything. Just enough to

hold your ground if someone attacks. Besides, Father's men won't let you near fighting. I overheard

him reminding Lord Gunther today."

"All right then. Again." Lucie once again placed her feet into position.

At end of the morning, Lucie was aching and covered in dust and sweat, but confident that she could

at least swing the sword without hurting herself.

"We'll have another practice before you go," Celine assured her. Lucie brushed escaping strands of

hair back and wiped her damp face with the corner of her tunic. Celine's smooth hair and

embroidered tunic were still pristine, not even marred by a tiny wrinkle. The only sign Celine had

practiced at all was the fine layer of dust coating her polished leather boots.

She held out a hand to Lucie. Together they went back to the castle.

CHAPTER NINETEEN

The horse's breath rose in the chilly air, puffs of steam hovering above the courtyard. There was a
smell of oiled leather in the crisp air. The sounds of clanking armour and rumbling voices punctured
the morning stillness. The raiding party was on its way, leaving a woebegone Celine gazing
mournfully after them.

Cowed by the noise and tumult of forty soldiers, Lucie took comfort knowing the familiar presence
of Red was nearby. Under his instruction, she found her way to the kitchens and finagled provisions.

She had taken enough to slip extra rations in her pack and even sneak Red a full pack of supplies.

Lucie, dressed in a soldier's tunic under her armour, rode in the middle of the group. To avoid
alerting the citizens that anything unusual was afoot, King Erich wanted it to appear that they were
merely offering relief to the outpost on the northern border.

The contingent was led by Lord Gunther, still grumbling about the lack of war. Despite this, Lucie
warmed to the big bear of a man whose gruff manners only thinly covered the fact that he had a

heart of gold. Despite Gunther's fierceness, she noted how his men deferred to him even when out

of his presence.

Halfway to Annecy, the sun started to set, its red glow covering them like a blanket. The party set up

camp in a large meadow. Lucie hovered awkwardly until one of the soldiers took pity on her,

handing Lucie a bulky canvas package wrapped with a twist of rope. After a long struggle, Lucie

managed to set up the tent which sat lopsided, like a crooked tooth in the tidy row of white squares.

"One of my men could have done that for you," Gunther said. He strode across the clearing, his

hulking figure towering over the rest of the soldiers.

Lucie proudly pounded in the past tent peg into the ground before she stood up, brushing stray grass

from her tunic. "It's all right, I'm sure they have plenty of work already."

"Well, come and eat then," he encouraged. Lord Gunther put a bear-like hand on Lucie's shoulder,

guiding her to the dining area. At the mess station he procured her rations: a chunk of bread and a

bowl of savoury stew.

"Sit," Gunther ordered, patting the ground next to him. Lucie plopped down breathing deeply as

steam scented with rich gravy curled into the brisk air. She scooped her bread in the stew and took a

large bite.

"We'll reach Annecy mid-afternoon tomorrow; from there we'll need you to direct us," he said.

Gunther dug into his stew, blew away the steam before shovelling it into his mouth.

Nerves jangled in Lucie's stomach. "Are we travelling directly through Annecy or around?"

"Through. There's the new outpost King Erich's building on the edge of the village. We may recruit some of their soldiers for backup if they have men to spare," Gunther stated.

Lucie swallowed hard, her food suddenly losing its flavour. "Wonderful," she said, her voice high and squeaky. Maybe no one will recognize me in the soldier's uniform, she convinced herself. Deep down, she knew this was unlikely.

Lord Gunther swallowed another huge spoonful of stew and washed it down with a swig of liquid from his flask.

"I know Erich's told you this already, but when we get to the bandit camp, you stay in camp," he said.

Lucie nodded, needing no reminder that her woeful swordsmanship would be no match for the bandits. "I can do that," she agreed.

"Good," Lord Gunther said. He polished off the rest of his stew and sauntered off in search of more food.

After a long night of tossing and turning on the lumpy bedroll, Lucie rose bleary-eyed and sleepy.

Overnight, the weather had turned; rumbling clouds hung low in a dreary grey sky and a faint drizzle threatened to turn into rain at any moment.

Lucie winced, climbing back into her saddle. The long ride yesterday left every muscle tender and

sore. The weather had King Erich's men subdued. It was a less boisterous group that made their way

into Annecy that afternoon.

Just great, market day, thought Lucie as they clattered toward Annecy Market Square. Even with

awful weather, the market was busy, the main street and the square thronged with venders and

buyers alike. Lucie shrank deep into the hood of her cloak attempting to avoid the curious stares of

the townspeople. She desperately hoped her uniform and cloak would be enough to blend in with

the raiding party.

The party rode through Annecy without incident, until a cry of panic sounded. Lucie heard it, high

and shrill over the commotion of men and horses. A small boy scampered away from his mother's

clutching fingers and was running straight in front of the horses. A usually placid war horse,

unaccustomed to small children, spooked and shied away, narrowly missing the tiny child. The boy

tumbled in a heap on the cobblestone street.

Lucie was closest, so without thinking, she slid down from her horse and ran to the little boy,

dragging him from underneath the pawing hooves. Standing up shakily, she handed him over to the

outstretched arms of his mother, who was pale with fright.

"Lucie?" Their eyes met, the boy's mother staring at her in shock. Morgan, Liliana's cousin, a girl

Lucie played with often in her childhood days. "What are you doing with those soldiers?"

"Don't tell anyone I'm here," Lucie said, putting her finger to her lips. Her eyes frantically darted

around the square. Her heart sank, the incident had already drawn a crowd. A sea of curious faces

with Lucie the centre of their attention.

"It's Lucie!" cried Morgan, ignoring Lucie's shushing gesture. "She's back."

Lucie groaned as the crowd of onlookers gathered closer.

"What are you doing here?" Izzie, narrowed her eyes, clutching her overflowing market basket in

one hand and a sack of onions in the other.

"I can't believe you'd show your face here again!" Ignoring the soldiers, Anton, a grim-faced trader,

one of the men who helped torch Lucie's cabin, pushed his way to the front of the throng.

Lucie stumbled back, eyes flashing to Gunther and his soldiers as angry townspeople pressed round

her.

"Stop!" Lord Gunther's commanding voice boomed, freezing everyone in their tracks. "This woman

is under King Erich's protection. If you take offense, you may take it up with him."

The townspeople drew away, muttering, but giving Lucie some breathing room. Izzie scrambled back

so quickly she dropped her bag of onions sending them rolling into a muddy puddle.

"As such, you will treat her with respect," Lord Gunther continued, letting his prancing war horse paw the ground. Anger glinted in eyes and his voice. "Anyone who doesn't will answer to me. And

King Erich."

Gunther pierced Anton with a fierce glare, then held out a hand to Lucie. In one swift move, he drew

her into the saddle in front of him. His weight was safe against her back. Solid.

"Lucie's a criminal," Anton protested, face indignant, resentment pouring off him. "Dangerous. She

broke into our cell and helped someone escape."

"Did she?" a smile played about Gunther's lips. "What proof of crime do you have? Whose cell did

she allegedly break into? The town buildings belong to the Crown."

Anton's mouth snapped shut and he stepped back, sulking. His wife elbowed him in the side, slicing

him a sharp look.

"Didn't you hear?" she whispered at her sullen husband. "Lucie's under the protection of King Erich.

Stop causing trouble."

Relief slithered up Lucie's spine as Anton allowed his wife to pull him, albeit reluctantly, away from

Lucie. Gunther emphasized his point, driving his horse forward, just a touch, causing the

townspeople to scurry back nervously.

"Does anyone else have something to report?" He looked pointedly at the trader who wisely

remained silent.

"Right," Gunther continued. "Now that the matter is settled, why don't you thank this young lady for saving your child and we'll be on our way."

"Th-thank you," stuttered Morgan, bobbing her head in Lucie's direction.

Lucie nodded in acknowledgement, noting the little boy had curled up in his mother's arms, thumb

tucked securely in his mouth. As long as the child was safe, Lucie was content.

"If anyone else wants to say something about Lucie, say it directly to me." Lord Gunther glowered at

the crowd of onlookers who quickly dispersed. Lord Gunther directed his horse to re-join his men.

"Thank you," Lucie said. She twisted in the saddle and gave Gunther a grateful look.

"Nothing to thank me for," Gunther rumbled. "Nothing worse than a group of ignorant, stubborn

people. They come from all walks of life."

"That's for sure," Lucie agreed, wiping a stray raindrop from her face.

It rained steadily throughout the afternoon, turning into a steady downpour by the time they made

camp. The rumble of distant thunder closed in as Lucie struggled to erect her soggy tent. Finally, one

of Gunther's men noticed her paltry efforts and helped her. Looking forward to dry shelter, Lucie

collected her camp rations — with weather like this, there would be no cooking — and crawled in

her tent. Quickly she peeled out of her wet clothes before swallowing her bread and cheese and

tucking her aching body into the bedroll.

Hours later, she was jerked out of her slumber when, above the beating rain and rumbling thunder,

a deep growly voice called her name.

"Who is it?" Lucie mumbled, sleep fogging her voice as she lifted the flap of her tent, peering

through the downpour. It was pitch black; Lucie couldn't even see her hand in front of her face.

"It's me, Red."

Lucie jumped at the deep voice not three feet away from her.

"How did you get into camp? Gunther has guards posted," she said quietly. Lucie grabbed her

waterlogged cape and squashed her feet into sodden boots.

"Don't come out, you'll be soaking. Can I come into the tent? The guard will be making his round

soon. I don't want to be seen."

"Of course, just let me move my bedroll," she said. Lucie scrambled to make space in the cramped

tent.

Red crouched down, carefully maneuvering himself into the tent, bringing a waft of woodsy

evergreen and smoke with him.

"It's not hard to sneak around the guard," Red explained, folding himself into a corner of the tent.

"They make the rounds exactly every hour and always the same pattern. Besides, they can't hear me

above the rain." He looked down ruefully, water ran off him in rivulets, dripping to form a muddy

puddle on the ground.

"I'm glad you made it through Annecy. Did the townspeople give you any trouble?"

"Well, there was an ... incident, but Gunther helped. He didn't let anyone near me," she told Red.

Red laughed softly. "Gunther's tough, but he's a good one to have on your side. He has a soft spot

for the underdog. Ahem, I mean he likes people to be fair." Red rushed to correct himself when an

offended look flickered across Lucie's face.

"I wasn't sure about Gunther at first, but he's definitely endearing himself to me," admitted Lucie.

"His men all love him. He reminds me of my father. He was the same with the men travelling in his

caravans."

"Gunther's always been a favourite, especially with the army. King Erich says he's one of the best

strategists he's ever seen. That's why he's always chosen for these kinds of jobs. You should see him

with a sword on horseback." Red let out a low whistle. "Lightning."

Lucie cleared her throat as Red eyes drifted, reminiscing. "That's wonderful, but we need to plan

how I'll find the bandit camp. I have the worst sense of directions, remember?"

"Yes, right, directions." Red shook his shaggy head sending droplets spraying around the tent. "I can

leave you clues."

"Clues?" Lucie raised an eyebrow.

"Yes, but they'll have to be subtle clues. I'll mark the trees. A cut about this height, so it'll be eye level on horseback." He raised a hand in the air to show Lucie what he meant.

"That could work," Lucie said. She nodded slowly, the weight of responsibility pressing on her chest

easing.

"Of course it'll work," Red declared. "If you start to go wrong, I'll lead you back in the right

direction."

A flash of lightning lit up the inside of the tent, followed immediately by a deafening clap of thunder,

making Lucie jump. "The storm is getting worse." She pressed a hand to racing heart. "Are you going

to be all right in that weather?" Lucie glanced around the tiny tent wondering if she could offer Red

her bedroll.

"Of course. I've seen much worse; and I'm more weather-proof than I used to be. I need to leave

now. The guard's due to come soon and I don't want to get caught. Can you look outside? Tell me

when the coast is clear."

Lucie opened the flap of the tent, peeking out, eyes straining through the downpour. Through the

darkness, a bobbing light approached. Lucie jerked the flap closed. "Get down! The guard's close,"

she whispered. Immediately, Red flung himself down, flattening his body to the floor of the tent.

"Lucie?" a voice sounded outside the tent, the spluttering torch cast flickering shadows through the

tent.

"Yes?" Lucie's voice was high with nerves.

"Are you all right, I thought I heard voices."

"Yes, everything's fine. I talk in my sleep sometimes," Lucie said. She held her breath as the light

gradually faded away, leaving the pair in darkness.

"That was close!" She inched the tent flap open. The guard's light was now a mere pinprick in the

distance. "The coast is clear." Lucie brushed a smattering of rain from her eyelashes.

Red pulled himself up off the ground. Pausing in the doorway, he took one last look over his

shoulder before loping away, disappearing into the dark forest.

By morning, everything was a sea of sticky mud. The rain was still coming down, now a fine mist

bleeding through the air, saturating it with fine droplets. Gunther's men huddled in damp groups

around smoky campfires, doing their best to stay warm. Lucie took a bowl of porridge finding a spot

next to Lord Gunther who was sitting on a damp log near his fire.

"We're close," Lucie said. She brushed off a moss-covered rock and sat down. "We should find the

bandits today."

"Good work," Gunther nodded approvingly, gulping hot tea from a steaming mug.

As Lucie scooped her spoon into the honeyed porridge, the gloomy silence was interrupted by a

clamour followed by a noisy scuffle. A distinctly feminine voice was complaining loudly. Lucy glanced up from her bowl as a group of solders came into view, urging a very reluctant, very damp, and very

bedraggled Celine in front of them.

"Celine!" Lucie's spoon clattered to the ground. "How did you get here?"

"I followed you of course. It's not like it was hard, there's forty of you and one of me," Celine said.

She swiped back a strand of hair, fierce determination shining from her eyes.

"Does your father know you're here?" Lucie asked.

"Well, he does now." The words hurtled from Celine's mouth, not a hint of remorse on her face. "I

left a note."

Gunther ran his hand through his shock of hair, tugging the ends in frustration. "You have to go

back." He clenched his teeth.

"No," Celine answered stubbornly, "and you can't make me. I outrank you." She lifted her chin, eyes

glittering.

"You did not pull rank on me," he stated.

Gunther gave the unrepentant girl a look of disbelief. She met his gaze evenly, lips pressed tightly

together.

"What if I did?" she replied. "I'm going to run this country someday. I need to start learning. Now

would be a good time."

Gunther sank back onto the log. "Your father is going to kill me for this," he muttered, his bushy

eyebrows drawn down in displeasure.

Celine beamed. "Does that mean I can stay?" she asked.

"Yes. But you're not fighting." His eyes slid fiercely to the sword hanging boldly from Celine's hip.

Celine pouted, before joining Gunther on his log. "Oh, come on Gunther. You know I'm good ...

better than most of you soldiers."

"No. Prancing round the practice ring is one thing but fighting, real fighting, is ugly. Besides, your

father would be furious. I'd lose my spot on the council. I'll be lucky if I don't end up in the dungeon

for letting you this far. If we weren't so close to our destination and I had men to spare, I'd send you

home immediately."

Celine's shoulders slumped in defeat as she kicked a pile of damp earthy smelling leaves. "Oh, all

right."

Lucie peered through the trees as she led the soldiers through the thick forest. Massive trees

loomed overhead, appearing larger than ever in the billowing mists. In spite of poor conditions, Lucie

vaguely recognized some landmarks: a twisting stream, an unusual rock jutting into the path, a giant

fallen tree, wet roots twisting into the sky. As he promised, Red slashed distinctive marks in regular

intervals for Lucie to follow.

"I think we're getting closer," she said to Gunther. "I can tell by these trees. And look over there."

She pointed at a large branch curving itself over a fern-filled gully. "I remember when we saw that

we were about ten minutes' walk away."

"Right," Lord Gunther said, pulling his horse to a stop, causing a flurry of activity as his soldiers

reacted to his sudden halt. "We'll send two men ahead, for reconnaissance."

"Oh, can I go?" Celine piped up, wriggling with excitement in her saddle.

"No," Lord Gunther said, studiously ignoring Celine's crestfallen expression. "It's far too dangerous.

Baines!" He barked an order at a nearby group of men.

"Yes sir." Baines stepped forward, snapping to attention.

"You're coming with Lucie and I to do reconnaissance," Gunther told him.

"Yes sir." Baine agreed with a grin, his eyes glinting with pride.

"Guard the princess at all cost. And don't let her sneak away," Lord Gunther ordered the rest of the

contingent, pointing to Celine, who was seated primly on a log with a huffy expression on her pretty

face.

Gunther gave Celine one last stern look before he and the two others disappeared, swallowed by the

forest.

CHAPTER TWENTY

They travelled on foot, through mist that swirled into a thick soupy fog. The leaves were slippery, the earthy smell of rotting wood and mushrooms hung heavy in the damp air. The three picked their

way cautiously over slick rocks, wet leaves and through thick spiky underbrush. A few times, Lucie

nearly lost the trail, but managed to find it again, keeping track of the marks gouged into the trees.

"Almost there," Lucie whispered to Lord Gunther, spotting the trail the bandits used to go in and out

of camp. She pointed to signs of disturbance on the forest floor. The three crouched behind a thicket

of baneberry bushes, peering out cautiously; Gunther's sharp eyes roved the bustling campsite

taking in every detail.

"It's well guarded," Gunther said, indicating a few armed sentries placed strategically around the

campsite. "They've got archers on watch."

Lucie followed Gunther's eyeline to a tree at the edge of the campsite. An archer crouched, mostly

hidden on a makeshift platform.

"But we'll have the element of surprise," Gunther said. He edged back gingerly, Lucie and Baines creeping behind him.

The three were turning to go deeper into the forest, when rustling caught Lucie's attention. She

spun around and saw the figure of a man, bow slung over his shoulder appear out of the fog.

Lucie froze, but Lord Gunther and Baines sprang into action. Baines flew at the man in one deadly

leap, tackling him to the ground. Gunther's sword flashed as he pressed it against the man's neck,

cutting off his shout of alarm.

"We'll have to take him with us," Gunther said, a grim expression slashed across his face.

He forced the man flat to the ground with his knee. Baine tied his handkerchief around the man's

mouth and, with Gunther's sword digging into his side, they prodded him, stumbling, back to camp.

The man's eyes widened in apprehension when he saw the clearing. Full of tents, soldiers, weapons.

Rope was quickly produced, as they tied him up securely.

"Please, don't hurt me," the man said, struggling and squirming when they loosened the

handkerchief from around his mouth.

Lord Gunther glared at the man. "Give me one reason why I shouldn't run my sword through you

right now. You came into our country looting, killing innocent citizens. Tell me who's behind this."

His fiery eyes bored into the man's face.

The man's face filled with terror. "I can't tell you. They'll kill my family. I have children."

Lord Gunther nodded shrewdly. "Admirable. But I have a duty to my soldier. If you're not useful, I
should probably just kill you now." He lifted the sword over his head to strike.

"No, wait — please!" the man cried, panic-stricken.

Lord Gunther lowered his sword a few inches, raising an eyebrow.

"Just—just make sure they don't know it was me," the man said.

Lord Gunther lowered his sword a few more inches. "Make sure who doesn't know?" Gunther
pinned him with a savage gaze.

"Penelope. She sent us," he gabbed, fear leaking from every pore. "She told us if we came and
destroyed the caravans, the trade, she would take care of our families. I didn't have a choice. Things
are bad in Iaisa. It was either do Penelope's bidding or starve. It's the taxes, even landowners can't
make a living. It doesn't help that everyone who is able is forced to work at the harbour digging. Or
on the ship building. There's no one left to work the land anymore. I couldn't let my wife and my
daughters starve." He looked pleadingly at Lord Gunther.

"Why did she send you?" asked Lord Gunther. HIs face was so expressionless. Lucie didn't know if
the woeful tale affected him or not.

"I don't know," the man said. He hesitated, a strange expression flitting across his face. "I think it's
the trade. Penelope wanted the trade for Iasia. It's all the new navy ships she built. She needs to pay

for them." The man's voice was pitched high with fear; his panic-stricken eyes focused on Lord Gunther's gleaming sword.

Gunther lowered his sword gradually. "I'll give you mercy," he said, "if you tell me everything, and I mean everything, about that camp. And don't think I'm freeing you; you're coming back to Carvon with us. King Erich will be extremely interested to hear your information."

After thoroughly extracting every bit of intelligence possible from their unwilling prisoner, Gunther drew Lucie aside.

"I'm tying him up and leaving him here with you and Celine. Judging from what he divulged, the camp outnumbers us, but most of them won't be armed when we attack. They're lazy and confident after being here unbothered. My men can take them, but only if we attack immediately, before he's missed. Just keep an eye on Celine. Make sure she doesn't slip off. The prisoner won't trouble you, he's well secured." Gunther eyeballed the prisoner, who was huddled under a dripping branch and muttering to himself.

"Are you sure you trust him?" Lucie glanced back at the prisoner. Lucie hadn't watched an interrogation before, but something seemed too easy.

"I don't trust anyone, but he's tied up too tight to move," Gunther said.

Gunther gathered his men and left with them. Only the constant dripping of rain broke the silence.

Celine kicked a nearby clod of mud, eyes glued longingly down the trail.

"I wish I could go too. I'm as good a fighter as any of them," Celine said.

"You are pretty good," Lucie said, settling by the smoking fire. "Just wait a few years. They'll have to

include you in things sometime."

"Not if Father has his way," Celine muttered. "He wants me to be safe, but he never allows me to do

anything." Her face clouded. "It wasn't like that before Frederich..."

"Disappeared?" Lucie rummaged through a pack, hoping to find tea leaves.

"Yes," agreed Celine. "He would have let me come. I know he would. Frederich always told me to

keep practicing, even when mother and father disapproved."

"Well, it looks like you kept up with it." Lucie spotted the tea under a package of dried beef and

spooned some into the kettle.

Celine cheered a little as she threw Lucie a cheeky smile. "I sneak into the arena early, you know. No

one's said anything to father about it yet either."

"Ahh..." Lucie put the kettle over the fire. "That explains a lot."

"Well, if he wants me to be safe, I have to defend myself." Celine set her jaw stubbornly.

A strange rustling, scraping sound behind the two girls cracked the silence. The girls jerked their

heads up in unison, eyes alert.

"What was that?" Lucie asked, whirling to search for the source of the noise.

"Look. Over there!" White-faced, Celine pointed a trembling finger toward their prisoner. "Is he ...

growing?"

Lucie's mouth rounded in a silent "o" as she stared in shock. That strange tingling sensation

thrumming over her skin. The man stretched, his flesh almost liquid, so long and thin he was nearly

transparent. The girls froze, too astonished to flee as he writhed, his body nearly the height of the

branches. He flicked, sliding loose ropes from wrists and ankles. A blink and he returned to his

normal size, eyes gleaming in triumph.

"How?" Celine's voice trembled, her whole body shaking.

"Magic," the man smirked, stepping toward the girls. "We still practice in Iasia you know. As it turns

out, the magic didn't stop when I crossed the border."

He took another menacing step toward them. Lucie stumbled back, nearly scorching herself on the

fire. Without warning, he pounced, grabbing Lucie around the neck, squeezing. Lucie's eyes felt like

would burst from their sockets as she fought to ease the pressure. She struggled, black spots

swimming before eyes, blood pounding like a hammer through every vein in her body. She choked,

helpless as his hands relentlessly crushed the delicate flesh. Lucie flailed, kicking uselessly at his

shins.

"Not so high and mighty now," he cackled as Lucie's vision blurred and faded.

A howl distracted him, enough for Lucie to suck a breath of desperately needed air into her lungs.

Out of the corner of her eye, she saw Celine, whirling a sword over her head. The man spun, trying uselessly to dodge her sword while keeping his hold on Lucie. It was as if time slowed. Celine's sword sliced his side leaving a gaping wound, he howled in pain and fury. Lucie rolled away, sucking in another breath of air, coughing as it passed over her bruised throat.

"You devil," he shrieked, springing up, pointed an outstretched hand at the princess.

"No!" shouted Lucie. She reached into her boot, sliding out her dagger and let it fly. The man grunted as the dagger struck, falling to the ground as it punched him in the shoulder. Celine flew in one sweeping motion, gripping her sword tightly in both hands as she plunged. He twitched and was still, one arm stretched out mid-growth, a shocked expression frozen onto his face.

Lucie hunched forward, head resting on her knees. "Are you all right?" she asked Celine.

The sword made a sucking noise as Celine pulled it out.

"I think so," Celine said. Her face was pale as she wiped the sword on the wet leaves before cleaning it on her tunic, leaving brown streaks of mud and blood on the hem. "I've never done that before."

Wobbling, she pressed trembling hands against her eyes.

Lucie wrapped a comforting arm around the younger girl, steering her away from the gruesome

sight.

"You were magnificent, Celine! You saved my life — and yours. He attacked first. You did what you

had to." Lucie comforted Celine, who looked on the verge of fainting.

"I know," admitted Celine, "but it feels wrong." She huddled by the fire, wrapping her arms around

her knees.

Lucie perched next to her, trying not to panic. How would Gunther's men survive if all the bandits

had magical abilities, she thought.

Hours later, the jangling of armour and horses interrupted their reverie. The raid was over. With

sadness, Lucie noticed a few men missing from the group. Others were nursing wounds.

"What happened?" Lucie jumped to her feet, searching for Gunther. He was at the back, supporting

Owen, who had an injured leg.

Gunther's expression was grim. "It didn't go well. I wasn't counting on the bandits being able to use

their magic in Lovan." He drew his black eyebrows down, perplexed. "Magic users haven't been able

to practice here for hundreds of years. I don't understand how this is possible. If we hadn't caught

them off guard, we would have been destroyed. Even so," he sighed, "if it wasn't for unexpected

help showing up, we would have been forced to surrender."

"Unexpected help?" Lucie and Celine hung on Gunther's words.

Gunther nodded. "A giant, too big to be human. The fog was so thick no one saw him clearly. He

appeared from the deep forest, fought fiendishly, then disappeared like a wraith just as the battle

ended."

Lucie kept her head down, eyes fixed on the leaves underfoot. Red? Her Red fought in the battle?

Her pulse thundered, wondering, worrying about his well-being. What if he were injured out in the

forest?

"Did anyone see him?" Celine's eyes brightened with excitement at this new development.

Gunther shook his head. "No, and I would have loved to thank him. Anyways, we'll to have to return

to King Erich. Immediately."

Gunther limped toward the smoking fire the girls had kept going. He glanced around, puzzled.

"Where's the prisoner?" he asked suspiciously.

"Umm... about that," Celine said, biting her lip. "He had magic too."

Lord Gunther swung his head, waiting for Celine to continue.

"He used the magic to break free, but we caught him," Celine finished quickly. "Unfortunately, he

didn't live."

Worry flashed through Gunther's eyes. "Did he hurt you?"

Celine shook her head. "He went after Lucie first and I took him with my sword," she told him, as

Lucie raised a hand up to the ugly bruises circling her neck.

A look of pride crossed Gunther's features, "Well done," he said. He patted Celine on the back with

his calloused hand. "It looks like your training paid off."

Celine's face glowed with pride at the compliment.

"What are we going to do now? We can't leave tonight," Lucie said.

Gunther rubbed his hands through his hair. "First, we'll post extra guards on duty tonight, in case

stragglers return. First thing tomorrow, we'll send word to King Erich. He'll call the council as soon as

possible. I still don't understand how the magic works here. For magic to work in any kingdom, it

needs a source. Lovan's source was destroyed hundreds of years ago. Everyone knows that."

Gunther's bushy eyebrows lowered in thought.

CHAPTER TWENTY-ONE

"A source?" Lucie turned to Gunther. Lucie's upbringing contained more fairy tales than history. She was, as most Lavonians, unfamiliar with the history of magic in Lovan.

"Yes," Lord Gunther explained. "Every country contains a magic source where mages and other gifted people draw energy from. The old Lavonian source was in the middle of the King's Forest, not too far from here. The mage guild maintained it in the old days. The Lavonian source was destroyed with the Lovanian mages. Surviving members of the mage guild scattered. The royal family couldn't – wouldn't – renew the source. Magic is dangerous in the wrong hands. They never restored the source. As a result, magic, all magic, was outlawed. Banned. Magic slips in …. occasionally. Fortune tellers, healers, small magic, but big magic can't be achieved without a source."

Lucie scratched her head, faintly recalling the demise of magic in Lovan from a history book Marion had forced her to read. "So, you're saying, if someone found the source, they could repair it and restore magic in Lovan?"

"Only someone extremely powerful and highly skilled. And obviously only King Erich and Queen

Isabella can reverse the ban. That's what we must resolve. How the bandits operated without a

source? We suspect Penelope is behind it, but we need proof. And to find out why she's hiding how

powerful she truly is. She must have accessed the source and used it."

Lucie caught her breath. The chateau. That must be the original source. Penelope was using it to

power her fiendish plan. Lucie fidgeted, gathering her courage to speak up.

"I think I might know where your source is," Lucie said.

"You do? Where?" Celine bounced on her toes excitedly.

"In the great oak forest, there's a chateau." Haltingly, Lucie explained what she knew about the

chateau – leaving out information about the Red.

"Can you lead us to the chateau?" Gunther asked, his eyes gleaming.

"I think so," Lucie replied, hoping she was doing the right thing. She was torn between her desire to

help and betraying Red's secret. "It's in the great oak forest, the king's forest, they called it in

Annecy. There's a man who lives there under a curse."

"Did Penelope curse him?" Celine's voice was hushed. She glanced around to make sure no stray

ears were listening.

"He never said it was Penelope's curse, but I suspect so. He was furious when I mentioned her, so I

never brought her name up again," Lucie answered.

"If Penelope is behind the bandits, we'll have to plan our moves carefully. We've suspected she's

more ambitious than she appears. That's why she was so determined to make the alliance with

Prince Frederich. We never suspected she would take her ambitions this far. If it's true she's

discovered or source, she's extremely dangerous," Lord Gunther said. He pressed his lips together

thoughtfully.

"Unfortunately, if she doesn't know by now that we're onto her treachery, she'll learn soon enough.

We must plan carefully and move immediately. Are you willing to lead us to this chateau?" Gunther

turned, waiting for Lucie's answer.

"Yes," Lucie agreed, knowing in her heart Red would understand. After all, Lovan was his concern.

CHAPTER TWENTY-TWO

"You're going to do what?" Red growled.

He had somehow sneaked past the extra guards Gunther had patrolling the campsite. Lucie nearly jumped right out of her skin when she heard him rustling at the tent flap.

"I'm sorry." Lucie lowered her lashes and squeezing her hands together in her lap "I thought it was the best plan. If we confront whoever did this. We'll reverse the curse, then you'll be free."

"Or make it worse," grumbled Red wolfing down the bread roll Lucie had filched from the camp rations.

"We have to at least try," Lucie pleaded. Her eyes shone in the faint light spilling into the tent. "If someone is using magic from the chateau as their source, turning it against Lovan, something has to be done. You can't just let her destroy everything without a fight. Then we can discover the secret to breaking your curse. Isn't that what you want?" Lucie's face softened.

Red chewed thoughtfully, a pensive look in his eyes. "And you want to help break the curse? My curse?"

"Of course I do," Lucie said. She reached out, laying a hand on his hairy arm and breathing in the

familiar smell of pine and smoke wafting around him. "We're friends — aren't we?" She quirked an

eyebrow.

"I guess it can't hurt to try," Red agreed, rubbing his hands over his face. "But just the chateau, I

don't want anyone to see me."

They spent two long days lingering in the wet, drizzly campsite waiting for reinforcements to arrive.

Lucie was more than ready to resume her journey. They had sent the reluctant Celine back to the

castle with the messenger, leaving Lucie feeling alone. She watched Celine leave, standing under the

trees until her horse disappeared into the depths of the forest.

"Unbelievable!" Lord Gunther's voice was filled with awe as the familiar iron gates of the chateau

came into view.

Lucy had to admit, the chateau was a magnificent and welcome sight. Rows of windows reflected

the setting sun and the pristine gardens were lush against the backdrop of the giant oak trees.

"I've heard of this place, but never imagined it existed," Gunter said. He turned to check on his men,

struck silent by the magnificent sight.

Leaving the others, Lucie led Gunther up the wide steps to the grand entrance. Just as she raised her

hand to the brass knocker, the door heaved open. She was nearly barrelled over in a flurry of rustling skirts.

"You're back!" Overjoyed, the usually reserved Katherine flung herself at her sister. Jasper wound

around her ankles in his own greeting. Lucie laughed, untangling herself from Katherine's

enthusiastic embrace.

"Katherine, this is Lord Gunther," Lucie said. She gestured toward Gunther, who after a week

traipsing through muddy forests was more than a little bedraggled.

Katherine curtsied prettily as Gunther's mouth dropped open. "Your sister?" he turned to Lucie,

brows lowered. "You didn't tell me your family was here."

"Ahh ... yes. We had to leave the village abruptly, so we came here. Red invited us," Lucie explained

to Gunther, who simply shook his head in bewilderment.

"Come inside," Katherine said, stepping aside. "Marion and Father will be dying to see you and Fleur

hasn't been the same since you've left."

"Your father's here too?" Flabbergasted, Gunther turned to Lucie. "Anything else you need to tell

me? Grandparents? Aunts? Uncles?"

"I'll explain inside." Lucie waved for Gunther to follow her into the chateau.

Leaving his men to set up camp and care for the horses, Gunther followed the sisters into the

chateau. He stared in astonishment when Fleur breezed over, tugging at his coat.

"I can't believe it," he said. Again, he stared, mesmerised, as a cup of tea and plate of delicate raspberry filled tarts floated over, settling on an inlaid table. "Do you know how all this happened?"

The girls shrugged. "They won't, or can't tell us. I honestly don't think they really even know

themselves," Lucie answered.

"You know nothing about how they arrived here? And what put them in this state? What about the

man you call Red, the one under the curse? Where is he?" Gunther skimmed the room, hoping to

see some sign of him.

"He doesn't want to meet anyone yet," Lucie explained, nibbling at her tart. "I'm hoping he'll come

around soon."

"Well, what can you show me? Have you learned anything about this chateau? Maybe from the

library?" Gunther asked, suspiciously studying the tart presented on a small plate before taking a

careful bite. Deciding it was safe, Gunther tossed the whole thing into his mouth, before swiftly

choosing another.

"The mirror," said Lucie, eyes gleaming. "That might help you."

"Mirror?" Surprise flitted across Katherine's face.

"Yes, a magic mirror. It's inside a secret room in the library. I didn't have time to show you before we

left. I'll take you there it now," Lucie said.

Lord Gunther snagged another pastry as they left the room, giving the plate a longing glance before

following Lucie down the maze of corridors. Lucie strode through the library, straight to the secret door.

"It's in here," Lucie explained, removing the books and hiding the secret lever. "As far as I know it

has always been here. This room isn't like the rest of the chateau, it is much older." She shivered.

The door swung open to reveal the mirror gleaming despite dust motes swirling in the musty air.

"I've heard about this artifact," Gunther said. Dazzled by the shining object and the history behind it,

Gunther carefully reached out to touch the mirror before deciding against it and pulling his hand

back.

"You can use the mirror to see things," Lucie explained. "I'll show you." She closed her eyes,

concentrating for a moment.

"Show me Celine," Lucie commanded. As she opened her eyes, the mirror clouded; from its depths

emerged Celine. She was whirling through the practice arena, shining sword flashing as it flew

through the air.

"See?" Lucie turned to Lord Gunther and Katherine, who gave her blank looks.

"I didn't see anything," Katherine said. A puzzled expression flitted across her face. She turned to

Lord Gunther, who nodded in agreement.

"Neither did I," Gunther admitted.

"Oh," Lucie deflated. "Well, maybe it will work if you try yourself."

Lord Gunther stepped up to the mirror obediently. Imitating Lucie, he closed his eyes. "Show me

King Erich," Gunther spoke in a loud voice. He opened his eyes and peered closely at the mirror,

which stubbornly reflected his face. He turned toward Katherine. "You try," he told her.

"Show me Mary," Katherine said and opened her eyes. This time the mirror wavered, a ripple in her

reflection, a mere hint of a blur before returning to stillness.

"I don't understand," Lucie said, pinching her nose in frustration. "The mirror has always worked

before. Can you try one more time?" She turned to Lord Gunther, who regarded the mirror

thoughtfully, running his finger around the distinctive design carved into the frame. Gunther

squeezed his eyes shut.

"Show me Penelope." His face creased in concentration.

Instantly, the mirror crackled. A violent energy churning underneath its polished surface. Eddies of

power unfurled from the depths. The hair on the back of Lucie's neck stood at attention.

"I thought you'd never ask!" A voice, powerful, melodious, yes somehow insidious in all its beauty,

rang out. It seemed to be echoing from a dark spinning cloud in the mirror.

Lucie felt a burning tingle sweep through her body and gasped in dismay as she clutched Katherine's

hand and took a hasty step back. A relentless tugging, pulling her innards toward the cold centre of

the mirror, dragged her relentlessly toward the object.

"Help," Lucie cried, struggling to keep balance. Her feet scraped against the stone floor. Katherine

grasped at her hand, but her efforts were useless. Lucie's hand slid away. She was pulled even faster

toward the mirror.

Lucie glanced frantically toward Gunther, who stood frozen, black hair standing out from his head in

a cloud of wires. She braced herself, preparing to slam into the hard, icy surface. Closer and closer,

the magic dragged Lucie toward its glittering surface. Just when Lucie braced herself to slam against

cold hardness, her hand slipped through the mirror, like water rippling into the glass with a loud

sucking sound. The burning tingle had drummed into an inferno of pain dancing across Lucie's skin

like a swarm of bees.

"No!" Through a hazy cloud of confusion, Lucie heard a bellowing roar behind her. Red crashed into

the room with a bang, tearing headlong past Gunther and Katherine toward Lucie. He grabbed her

hand tight, pulling her back from the mirror. Lucie yelped in pain. It felt like she was being torn in

two.

Suddenly, the tension eased. All was darkness as the mirror swallowed them both. Lucie panted in

relief from the sudden lack of pressure. A faint light gleamed behind her. Lucie turned. It was like

swimming underwater. She saw the dim, wavering figures of Katherine and Lord Gunther through the glass, mouths hanging open in shock. Then everything disappeared in a flash of light. Lucie and

Red tumbled onto a polished marble floor in a vast airy room.

Blinking in the harsh brightness, Lucie took in her surroundings. At one end, white marble steps led

up a dais to an enormous throne. The room was lined with tall glass windows. Lucie glimpsed

looming snow-capped mountains engulfed by thick forest.

Then the beautiful lilt of that musical voice dragged Lucie's attention away from the landscape.

Behind her, adjacent to an ornate mirror, a mirror identical to the one Lucie was moments before

swept into, stood a beautiful woman. She was so beautiful it hurt to look at her.

The woman smiled, shaking her head as she gave the pair a pitying look. "Still haven't broken that

spell yet?" She directed her question to Red, who was still slowly getting to his feet.

"And you," she said. She glided toward Lucie, a river of shining hair floating behind her. "You are

quite the little busybody, aren't you?"

Lucie cowered at the icy tone penetrating the woman's voice. "Don't think there aren't

consequences for your little games." She smirked, toying with a gem-encrusted sceptre cradled in

her delicate fingers.

Lucie narrowed her eyes, gaze darting past the woman toward a door behind the marble steps. Lucie inched forward, hoping Red would understand and make a dash with her.

"Uh, uh, uh!" The woman turned, flicking the glowing sceptre at Lucie. A streak of purple light shot

from its jewelled tip. Lucie felt the now familiar tingle of magic wash over her, making her limbs cold

and sluggish.

"What is it you want, Penelope?" Red stepped protectively in front of Lucie, towering over the

woman with his impressive height. Lucie blinked slowly, watching the pair struggling to keep her

head upright. It felt like she was encased in thick, sticky syrup.

"Oh my, we're certainly protective," Penelope said. Her eyes turned cold as she fingered the shining

object in her hand. "Funny, when I needed something, you weren't nearly so helpful."

"You know I couldn't go along with your intentions," Red glowered, taking a menacing step forward.

"You would enslave the entire kingdom of Lovan, just to expand Iaisia. Your plan was to cause chaos

and destruction. To my people."

"Not enslave – improve." Penelope's voice took on that mesmerising lilt. Lucie shook her head,

trying to focus; clear the fuzziness.

"Give them opportunities they never dreamed of," Penelope said. "Yes, at a cost, a temporary cost."

She twirled the sceptre, causing streaks of light to escape and shine across the smooth marble floor.

"My plans would have changed everything for the better."

She whirled, glaring at Red. Fury ignited in her eyes and her hair whipped around in a wild cloud.

"You had to ruin everything with your old-fashioned morals. We could have had everything and then she came along." Penelope stopped pacing long enough to shoot a vicious look at Lucie. "This little nobody. Suddenly you had time. You listened. Don't think I wasn't watching you two."

Lucie forced her eyelids to stay open, fighting to comprehend the words as a heavy wave of sleepiness swept over her. Her chin dropped to her chest; black spots swam before her eyes.

"Lucie?" Red's voice drifted faint, distant. "Lucie?"

"I'm fine," she mumbled, but her head felt like it was stuffed with wool. "Just need a.... little.... rest."

Her head slumped to the icy floor, but she barely noticed as her eyes drifted shut.

"No! Lucie! Stay with me, don't go to sleep," Red said, shaking her by the shoulder.

Lucie battled against another wave of sluggishness that swelled through her. Her mind struggled through a thick haze to understand what was happening.

Red growled deep in his throat, leaping at Penelope, hands outstretched. Silken hair flying, she danced back, perching on the arm of the white throne.

"Not so fast," she said, her red lips curved in a smile.

Red hurled himself at Penelope again. But in a swish of satin, she appeared at the other end of the hall, stepping from a thin twist of smoke that hung in the air like gauze.

"You thought you were strong, so much better than me," Penelope's voice echoed, flitting away

each time Red got close. "Breaking our alliance for the good of your people. Ha! They don't know

what they're missing. That Alliance was the beginning of marvellous things for everyone. We could

have ruled the world together. But you just had to listen to your morals," Penelope spat the words

with venom. "How dare you? No one says no to me."

Wait, what? A pinprick of realization forced its way through Lucie's fog. Red, her Red was Frederich?

She should have known all along, Lucie thought. She forced her eyes open just to see him once again

fling himself at Penelope. He was thwarted when she skipped away in her deadly game of cat and

mouse.

"Too late now," Penelope said.

Glee crossed her face as she waved the sceptre. It glowed fierce and hot. She stalked toward Lucie,

flicking it at Red in a shower of sparks when he got too close. He watched, helpless as Penelope

skimmed across the polished floor, her eyes fixed on the helpless girl.

Lucie, despite her confusion, knew the danger and struggled to lift her head from the icy floor, but

her muscles refused to obey. She collapsed into a boneless heap.

"No!" Red roared, diving toward Penelope. He clawed at the trailing hem of her dress and she shrieked, tumbling to the floor. Just as he wrestled the sceptre from her grasping hand, she bit him

in the arm. The sceptre clattered to the floor, rolling slowly, slowly across the floor.

"Lucie, get the sceptre," Red bellowed, struggling to pin down the writhing, spitting Penelope.

Not able to stand, Lucie struggled to her knees, dragging herself across the floor. Slowly, she pushed

through the glue of Penelope's spell, inching closer to the sceptre. Behind her, Penelope screeched,

realising what was about to happen. Lucie edged her hand toward the sceptre, which was still

vibrating, and wrapped her stiff fingers around cold metal.

Penelope howled as Lucie closed her hands around the heavy sceptre. The magic surged through

her, instantly clearing all confusion. Every nerve tingled with pulsing energy. Lucie stood tall,

gripping the sceptre tightly in her fist as Penelope froze.

"Noooo!" Wailing, Penelope wrenched free from Red's grip spring at Lucie, vicious hands raised. In

one violent motion she swiped the sceptre from Lucie, raising it high above her head.

Penelope's features twisted with a vengeance. She closed her eyes, and the wand glowed. The light

was so intense Lucie had to turn or be blinded by its white hot power. As she raised her hand to

strike, Red vaulted across the floor and flung himself in front of the surging bolt of energy. Lucie

toppled back, shocked, as Red twitched and lay still.

CHAPTER TWENTY-THREE

Lucie froze, staring at the body stretched out on the floor. Red's body.

Grief.

Dread.

Terror.

Sadness engulfed her in a tide. To her disbelief, his body writhed, shrinking, its form twisting and shifting. To her shock, alarm cracked his icy features. Stricken, Lucie lifted her eyes toward Penelope.

"This shouldn't be happening," Penelope whispered, her voice full of horror.

The form on the floor continued moving, finally settling with a shudder. Eerie stillness filled the room. Unable to tear herself away, Lucie glued her eyes to the figure on the floor.

His eyes opened. *Blue eyes. He's handsome.* Lucie thought. He sat up, shielding his face from the light.

Penelope stepped back, her face incredulous, as Red, who was not Red anymore, stood. She raised her sceptre to strike him, but the violent light radiating from it subsided to a spluttering glow before completely fizzling out. Red reached out, taking the sceptre from Penelope's trembling fingers.

"My Father and your council will be interested in your thoughts on this matter," he said. Frederich tapped the now quiet sceptre against his hand. Penelope opened her mouth to reply, but no sound came out. Red reached out to grab her arm, but in a flurry of silk, Penelope was gone, leaping toward the tall window. In one swoop, she flew, balancing on the windowsill before plunging into a billow of thick smoke.

Lucie and Red darted to the window, peering over the sill. They saw only a flock of seagulls cawing in the distance.

Lucie perched on the bottom step of the dais, letting the enormity of it sink in. "So, you're..."

"Frederich. My sister called me Red when I was young. I didn't want to use my proper name when you arrived at the chateau; too dangerous... too hard to explain."

Frederich lowered himself next to her, baggy clothes flapping around his resized frame.

"When I learned Penelope planned to use the alliance between Lovan and Iasia to merge power and take over both kingdoms, among other things, I had to break the alliance. I saw how she treated the Iasians and destroyed the kingdom. I couldn't let that extend to Lovan."

"So that's when you broke the engagement? Did you know about Penelope's magic?" Lucie slid her eyes to the sceptre resting quietly between them.

"I suspected Penelope had considerably more power than she showed me, but I didn't know she had accessed the mirror and the sceptre. But I was too late. The engagement linked Penelope to Lovan, giving Penelope a toehold to bring magic in and restore the source herself. When Penelope discovered that I planned to break the engagement. She took matters into her own hands and escalated her plans. That's when she cursed me — forcing me to the chateau."

"And the chateau, it was the old source of magic in Lovan?" Lucie asked. Frederick nodded. "I don't know how she activated it, but I think it saved me. She didn't intend to let me live that day out."

"What happened in here then? What broke the curse?" Lucie peeked at Frederich, then lowered her lashes, a blush staining her cheeks. Frederich's new appearance still startled her.

"I'm not certain," he said. He contemplated the mirror, its icy surface reflecting the vast expanse around them. "I must have interrupted her curse somehow." He tugged his leather boots, now far too big for his human-sized feet.

"Oh." A breeze rustled through the open window, tickling the strands of hair escaping around Lucie's cheeks. Lucie shyly glanced at Red again. Prince Frederick, she reminded herself sternly, was strictly off-limits now that he was a prince again. She gave herself a little shake.

"What now?" Lucie didn't even know what kingdom she was in.

Frederich brushed himself off, taking one last look before they left the echoing room. "We decide what to do next. And return to Lovan as soon as possible."

"This place gives me the heebie-jeebies. Where is everybody?" Deadly silence surrounded them. The only sound was their own footsteps tapping down the empty corridors that stretched for miles. "Did you ever come here? You know, during the engagement?" Lucie asked.

"No." Frederich opened the door to yet another empty stateroom, its furniture a collection of ghostly shapes under their dust covers. "I've only been to Penelope's castle in Florin. I had no idea this estate existed. We must be somewhere west, in the Luman mountain range. They're the only Iasian mountains this size. If so, we're a few days ride from Lovan's western border." He opened the next door.

"What are we looking for?" Lucie peered around him.

It was a storage or laundry area. Stacks of linens were lined neatly on shelves. An enormous set of cupboards stood against the other wall.

"Clothes," Frederich said. He hitched up his loose trousers, heading for the armoires. The huge wooden doors creaked open. "Here we go."

The closet was stuffed full of clothes, including laundered uniforms. Frederich sorted through the piles, choosing serviceable-looking breeches and a mended tunic. In another cupboard, Lucie discovered a useful-looking satchel and two warm woolen cloaks.

"We need food too. Did you see the kitchens?" Lucie folded her loot in a pile, tucking it into the satchel.

"In Lovan, they're on the ground floor. Handier for deliveries and storage. I saw a servants' entrance behind us. That should lead there eventually," Frederich said. He headed toward a half-hidden staircase in a nearby alcove. Lucie followed, gripping tightly to the iron handrail as they made their way down the stone steps.

The smell of roasting meat eventually brought them to a large kitchen where half-prepared food lay scattered. A roast still turned on the spit above the fire, and a fragrant pot of soup was simmering on the range. Lucie picked up a roll stuffed with a spicy meat filling and examined it before taking a cautious bite.

"Tastes good," she said. She savoured the fresh taste of coriander and spice in her mouth. "Want one?" She held the platter out to Frederich.

"We need provisions, enough for a week," Frederich told her. He picked up a roll Lucie offered and bit into it.

"Let's see..." Lucie said as she hopped off the countertop and began hunting through cabinets. "Spicy sausage! Yum! Here's some cheese, too. Grab that bread over there." She gestured toward a rack of bread still warm from the oven. "I'll search the pantry. They might have useful things in there." Lucie busied herself searching through one of the pantries. "Oh, there's a lot of dried food here. Do you like lentils?" She popped her head out of the pantry.

"Yes, I could eat those," he said. Frederick joined her in the pursuit of suitable supplies for traveling.

"I wonder what happened to everyone." Lucie considered a bag of dried beans before stuffing them into the satchel with their other items. "Do you think they're here? Invisible – like the chateau? Maybe they're watching us right now?" Lucie shivered.

"I'm not sure," Frederick said as he pushed back his hair. "I'm finding out more and more that Penelope kept many secrets from me. You know how strict we are about magic in Lovan. No one is even allowed to learn magic except for a few members of Father's council."

"Is that why you didn't want anyone to know she cursed you?" Lucie set down her bulging satchel and swiped another of the meat rolls, wondering if she could figure out the recipe from the taste.

"Part of the reason. Father's always been against magic. He didn't want anyone to turn their magic against the family. It was the thing we argued about the most. Father eased his position a little when I left. I was afraid Penelope's curse would make him backtrack."

Lucie's hand paused halfway to her mouth. "Do you think they should allow magic in Lovan?"

"Well, if we could use magic ourselves, we could have avoided this whole debacle," Frederich remarked. He fastened his bag before hefting it onto his shoulder. "I have to convince Father now. I'm not sure the curse situation will help, but I have to try."

"Why?" Lucie looked around to make sure she had missed nothing essential they needed.

"Because I have good reason to believe there are mages in Lovan. And I don't think it is fair to take magic away from everyone because a few have misused their gifts."

"You think there are mages — in Lovan?" Lucie's eyes rounded. "What makes you think that?"

"First, it makes sense." Frederich unlatched the heavy wooden door leading to the kitchen garden, gesturing for Lucie to follow him. The crisp air and sunshine felt good after the stifling kitchen. "All the mages or anyone who could use magic. Their ability wouldn't just stop because we banned them from using magic anymore. It's in their blood."

"But didn't the source give them the gift?" Lucie asked. She plucked a sprig of rosemary, breathing in the clean scent.

"It helped, yes, but people have the gift inside of them. It is who they are." They crossed another courtyard, heading to the stable, a large low building clinging to the south side of the castle.

"Just because someone possesses a gift or ability doesn't make them evil. Not everyone is like Penelope."

"I suppose," Lucie said, chewing her lip. "So, you plan to convince King Erich to change the law? Lift the ban?"

"Something like that."

Lucie blinked when they entered the dim light of the stable, breathing in the warm, comforting smell of hay, horses, and leather. The horses had escaped whatever strange magic made all the people disappear. Their velvety noses poked over their stall doors and their liquid eyes were curious about the strangers entering their domain. Nearby, a small grey cat scampered off, surprised by their sudden entrance.

Frederich lost no time choosing two sturdy bays. He led them out of their stalls.

"What will happen to all the horses?" Lucie wondered, stroking the nose of a friendly brown mare.

"I'm not sure. We can put them into the pasture. They'll graze until someone comes for them. I'll help as soon as I finish saddling these two."

While Frederich finished preparing the horses, Lucie led the others, several companion ponies, and a small stubborn donkey into the pastures. They trotted away, happy in their freedom.

Now the castle was truly deserted. After one last check to ensure they had everything they needed, Lucie and Frederich rode down the winding track that led through the mountain range. The tightness that clutched Lucie's chest only loosened

when the mysterious castle disappeared into the distance behind them.

CHAPTER TWENTY-FOUR

"We're here!" An expression of mixed anticipation and apprehension crossed Frederich's face as familiar gates slowly opened. Wanting to see King Erich first, Frederich drew the hood of his cloak over his distinctive golden hair.

The guard, fooled by their servants' uniforms, only gave the pair a cursory glance before waving them through the stone arches. Frederich had kept his reappearance under wraps thus far by keeping a low profile, travelling through towns and villages at night, and keeping his hood up whenever they crossed paths with any other travellers.

"They'll be astonished to see you," Lucie said, forcing cheer into her voice over the sense of anxiety and sadness that wrenched her chest.

She wasn't looking forward to returning to her old life. As she glanced at Frederich, tall and proud in his saddle, she knew she was going to miss him. She tore her thoughts away as they clattered into the courtyard. This was Frederich's moment of happiness. She wouldn't ruin it for him.

One of the grooms met them. As his hand stretched to take the reins, Frederich drew back the hood of his cloak, revealing his face.

"Your Highness?" the groom exclaimed in disbelief.

"Hello, Gerhard," Frederich greeted him. He dismounted, handing the horses to the dumbfounded groom. Lucie stood awkwardly next to Frederich, wondering what she would do with herself now that he was safely home.

"Are you coming?" Ignoring the whispers of the crowd gathering around them, Frederich took her hand in his, leading her through the courtyard and straight into the castle.

Word spread quickly in the castle. Before they knew it, Queen Isabella was flying toward them at a print.

"Frederich!" Tears of joy spilling from her eyes as Queen Isabella threw herself into his arms, squeezing him tightly. Celine and King Erich followed her. "How is this possible?" the queen sobbed, wiping tears from her cheeks.

To her surprise, Frederich drew Lucie close to his side and tucked her under his arm. "I couldn't have returned without Lucie," he said.

"For that, we owe you everything," Queen Isabella said. She held out a hand, and Lucie took it shyly, suddenly aware of her windblown hair and clothes smelling of campfire smoke.

"Yes. We can't thank you enough!" King Erich inclined his head toward Lucie.

The comforting weight of Frederich's arm returned to Lucie's shoulders. She realized, for now, she was where she belonged.

CHAPTER TWENTY-FIVE

"Penelope's alive and free. We don't know where she is or what she's planning?" King Erich's face was grave, eyes shadowed. At Queen Isabella's insistence, tea and cake were served in the comfort of the royal apartments; Lucie felt out of place perched on a pristine velvet couch, luxurious finery surrounding her. "This is a worrisome development. We'll meet with my council early in the morning to discuss the next step." His cup clinked as he set it down firmly.

"Lucie, You've sacrificed so much for the Lovanian kingdom already—but would you mind accompanying Frederich in the morning to debrief the council?"

Lucie gulped, palms sweating. "Yes. Of course," she choked out. Frederich put a protective arm around her, pulling her close. Celine eyed his move, a speculative look flitting across her face.

"I take it since you're free from Penelope... the two of you...?" Celine smirked, raising an eyebrow. Lucie hastily scooted away from Frederich as if burned by a hot poker.

"Um... no." Lucie squeaked, cheeks blazing. Frederich cleared his throat, busying himself adding lumps of sugar in his tea.

A smile played around Queen Isabella's lips as she studied the blushing Lucie, who averted her eyes, twisting icy hands in her lap.

"Wait a minute." Celine broke the awkward silence, abruptly changing the subject. "Does this mean I don't have to be queen anymore?" She beamed around the room.

King Erich laughed, "Yes, you're off the hook, but you're still in a lot of trouble for that stunt you pulled, young lady. Speaking of which..." he turned to Lucie. "There are some people you'll want to see."

"Me?" Lucie jerked her head up, wondering who she could possibly know at the royal castle.

"Yes." King Erich gestured to a nearby aide. "Bring in Lucie's family."

Lucie's eyes rounded in surprise and delight as the aide opened the door, revealing Katherine, Marion, and Pierre, Lucie's Father. Forgetting her shyness, Lucie jumped off the couch, running toward her family.

"How did this happen?" she asked, overcome with emotion.

"It was an hour after you and Red disappeared into the mirror," Katherine explained. "Of course, we were frantic with worry about you two. But we had more to worry about when the entire chateau disappeared. One second the chateau was there, the next it was just.... gone. We were sitting in the middle of the forest under a giant oak tree, the ruins of an old castle lying all around us—the chateau. Only the servants remained, which is where it gets really strange. We *see* them now; the servants aren't invisible anymore. They *appeared*."

"Do you mean Fleur?" Lucie interrupted, forgetting in her excitement to be intimidated by the royal family surrounding her. "You see Fleur now?"

"Yes." Katherine nodded. "She'll be overjoyed that you're here and safe. Talked about you nonstop the entire journey."

"And the mirror? Did that disappear too?" Lucie held her breath, anxious for details.

"We looked everywhere, but we couldn't recover it—it could be in the ruins somewhere. They're *huge*; we never explored them—Gunther was rushing to return to the castle and report to King Erich. King Erich is sending men to the chateau site to investigate—make sure we missed nothing important."

"The spell on the chateau must have broken along with my curse. I wonder if that means the source isn't operational anymore," Frederich chimed in, eyes blazing with excitement.

King Erich shook his head, "Penelope must be truly powerful and determined if she could do all that."

"Well," Frederich said, "Less powerful now we have this." He reached under his cloak and pulled out the gleaming sceptre, sending an electric shiver running through the room. Queen Isabella's little dog cowered under the settee. "Penelope also used this as a source of power."

King Erich reached out, taking the sceptre in his hand, gently hefting the weight in his palm. "I never imagined the sceptre still existed. It must be thousands of years old. The Lavonian sceptre disappeared—or was hidden when magic was banned, no one knows what became of it." King Erich turned the object in his hand, the jewels shooting colourful reflections dancing across the walls. He handed it back to Frederich, "We'll have to be careful with it. As we know, it's extremely dangerous in the wrong hands."

Lucie, mesmerised by the beauty of the sceptre, leaned closer, reaching out to touch it—then snapped her hand back as the sceptre crackled. A tingle bolted through her fingers.

"What was that?" Lucie rubbed the stinging spot where her hand touched the sceptre.

"The sceptre responded to you." King Erich drew his brows down. "That shouldn't be possible... unless you're a mage or have magic in your blood somehow." King Erich threw Lucie an inquiring look. She shook her head. There was no magic in Lucie's family that she knew of.

"We'll have to research how the sceptre works—get expert advice." King Erich paused, contemplating the sceptre before gesturing toward the aide.

"Send word to Lord Remy immediately." Snapping a smart salute, the aide scurried out of the room to do the king's bidding.

"Of course, you must stay in the castle as personal guests—until the danger has passed." King Erich waved his hand, including all members of Lucie's little family. "Especially you, Lucie. We owe you everything for bringing Frederich back to us."

Before she knew it, Lucie was sinking down in a soft lavender-scented bed. Exhausted after days of travel, the warmth of the fire lulled her into a deep sleep, and she only woke when her sisters pushed their way into the stateroom.

"Tell us everything." Marion was brimming with enthusiasm and looked healthier than ever, gently rounded cheeks and shining hair demonstrating the result of nutritious food and excellent care.

Lucie sat, rubbing sleep from bleary eyes. "At least let me have a cup of tea first." Over three cups of jasmine-scented tea and an array of cakes and sandwiches, Lucie shared her story with Katherine and Marion.

"But when did you know Red was Frederich?" Marion prodded, picking icing from her petit four.

"I didn't know. Not until Penelope said it," Lucie said.

"You know he likes you." Katherine dropped another lump of sugar in her tea and stirred, the spoon clinking gently against the gold-rimmed cup.

"I don't think so, not like that anyway." Lucie protested, cheeks pinking. The blood pulsed in her veins at the thought. "He's grateful because he doesn't have to be 'Red' anymore."

"I've seen the way he looks at you. He can't tear his eyes off you," Marion argued. "And..." she paused meaningfully, "I think you were looking back. I don't blame you."

Lucie put her hands to her hot cheeks. "I can't help it. I know there's no point because he's the *prince*. Frederich's so kind and good to me. Even at the chateau—before we broke the curse. And how he's so..."

"Handsome?" supplied Katherine. She sipped from the dainty cup, pursing her lips as the hot liquid passed over them.

"Yes. *Now*, but if Red hadn't changed to someone so—if he wasn't *Prince Frederick. Crown* Prince Frederick. I might have a chance with him." Appetite gone, Lucie plopped down the tiny sandwich she was nibbling. "I wouldn't wish the curse back, but everything will be different between us now. And I never had time to tell him how I feel. I can't now. He'll think I'm doing it for his title." Lucie stared at the floral pattern on the rug, blinking hard.

"I don't know about that," Marion encouraged. "King Erich didn't seem to be poo-pooing you. The king and queen have a soft spot for you."

"Yes," scoffed Lucie. "*Now*, when King Erich's excited to have Frederich back. But give him a few weeks, and he'll come to his senses. I mean, King Erich has alliances to think about. Other countries besides Iasia that need alliances—Louixe for one. And, King Erich is anti-magic—and that sceptre seems to think I have the gift," Lucie whispered the last word, glancing up furtively as a knock at the door interrupted Lucie mid-sentence.

"You're required by Lord Remy in the library, Miss Lucie," a starched maid stood stiffly at the door.

Lucie halted at a set of double-height doors leading to the castle library. The maid rapped smartly. The door swung open, and Lucie stepped into the welcome smell of dusty books, immediately soothed. Opposite from the grandeur of the chateau library, the castle library was a far more utilitarian space. Lucie wondered how people ever found specific books. The maid led Lucie through leaning stacks, a haphazard maze of shelves stretching on indefinitely. Lucie craned her neck, gazing at the bookshelves—some towering two stories above her head. Eventually, they reached the back of the library, where the maid entered a small doorway, waving for Lucie to follow.

"Hello Lily, I'm Lord Rueben," a rotund man greeted Lucie effusively, taking her hand in both of his pudgy ones and shaking enthusiastically. Twinkling eyes behind round spectacles peered at her eagerly. "I hear you have magical talent. The *gift*.

Very strange. Very unusual indeed in Lovan." Lord Ruben nearly tripped over the words in his excitement. "Now. Come. Sit here." Lord Rueben moved a teetering stack of papers and waved Lucie to an overstuffed chair before plunking the papers onto an enormous pile of books.

"I'm Lord Remy, historian and magic expert. One of only two magic experts in the entire kingdom of Lovan." Lord Remy pushed up his gold-rimmed glasses, settling across from Lucie, one leg over a chubby knee. "I have to tell you, these are exciting times. *Very* exciting. Magic hasn't been used in Lovan for centuries, and now, it has suddenly reappeared. So delightful. I hear that you have an amazing talent for it—the *gift*. I can't wait to see what you offer—er—show me." Eyes gleamed behind the shining spectacles.

"It's not much," Lucie confessed, leaning against the cushioned seat, wondering if it would be terribly rude to tell him her name wasn't Lily. "I don't think I even have a real gift—I'm definitely not a mage. The only reason people think I'm gifted is because of the sceptre. When I touched the sceptre, it sparked."

"Yes." Lord Remy nodded encouragingly. "The sceptre would only react if it were responding to magic you already have. Tell me, is there any history of magic in your family?"

"I don't think so. Not that I know of. My father mentioned no gift—I never knew my mother, but my sisters did. They never mentioned the gift."

"What *can* you tell me about your mother?" Lord Remy tapped his fingers together under his chin.

"Very little," Lucie admitted. "My mother died when I was a baby. My sister, Marion, raised me from babyhood."

"Ahh... I see. Were your sisters able to perform magic? Did they mention magic or the gift to you?"

"No, not that I can remember." Lucie rubbed damp palms on her knees. Lord Remy's office was warm. She was starting to sweat.

"Well, I'll explain to you how the gift works; then maybe we can conduct some tests." Lord Remy reached for his ginger cake, taking an enormous bit. "As you know, Lovan bans magic—has for centuries."

Lucie nodded.

"But, as Prince Frederich informed you, we suspect some citizens still have magic in their blood—the *gift*. But they can't or aren't allowed to *use* it. The *gift* might show up as a talent or unusual quirk. Healing, seeing the future, things like that. Do you know anyone who does these things?" Lord Remy leaned forward, a glint of curiosity in his eyes.

"Well, Althea, from my village was good with herbs and healing." Lucie hesitated.

"Yes," Lord Remy wagged his head. "I think I may have heard of Althea. Is she from..."

"Annecy," Lucie supplied, looked around the room, noticing a shelf holding an odd, creepy assortment of objects above Lord Remy's head. An ornate dagger, some curious manuscripts, an ancient statue of a birdlike creature.

"Yes, someone like Althea. Their magic makes them excellent at what they do. But, the potent magic disappeared hundreds of years ago when the source was destroyed." Lord Remy frowned.

"So, how did the source of magic return to Lovan?"

"Now, this is the interesting thing, Lily." Lord Remy vibrated, trembling with excitement. "I have some theories. One theory is the alliance. Because Prince Frederich, who I hear you brought back to Lovan—well done, by the way—was engaged to Princess Penelope; it gave Penelope a legal entry point. Because the royal family destroyed the magic, only the royal family could bring magic back again. No Lovanian royalty restored the source—or had the ability to. Magic is, unfortunately, watered down in the royal blood." Lord Remy pursed his lips disapprovingly.

"The engagement, along with the fact that Penelope pinpointed the exact location of the ancient Lovanian source of magic. I haven't verified this with Frederich, but I'm guessing that place or a location near there is where she decided to cast her curse?"

"What exactly destroyed the source?" Lucie scrunched her eyebrows curiously.

"Three or four hundred years ago, there was an extremely evil, extremely powerful mage, Lord Malfoy. Lord Malfoy was a persuasive mage. From the history I've learned, many mages start good, but when they gain too much power, it goes to their head. This is what happened to Lord Malfoy. Lord Malfoy decided that since he was so powerful, he would challenge the king. A coup, so to speak. Malfoy planned to reign, not merely Lovan but all the surrounding kingdoms as well. A great battle followed. All the surrounding kingdoms joined, each bringing their most powerful magic. Before they finally defeated Malfoy, he had caused much devastation and enslaved and killed thousands. It was an epic fight, and in the end, it humiliated the royal family. Afraid it would happen again, they rid the Lovanian kingdom of all magic. I don't know how they accomplished this, and I don't think anyone remembers. The capital moved to Corvan—the old city burned to the ground in ruins. The royal family decreed that Malfoy's name would be forgotten, erased from history; mostly, it disappeared."

"Weren't there any good mages? They can't *all* be evil?" Lucie questioned.

"Of course, lots of good mages. Many mages were destroyed in battle or forced into hiding, only to disappear along with all their possessions. Priceless artifacts, gone forever." Lord Remy shook his head sadly.

"That's why the sceptre is such an exciting discovery." Lord Remy reached over the table, gently lifting a velvet-wrapped item from the mahogany desk. Slowly, carefully he unwrapped the material revealing the sceptre. Almost against her will, Lucie leaned forward to look at it, magic skimming her skin like a butterfly's caress.

"King Erich is the first king in centuries to even entertain the idea of lifting the magic ban in Lovan. He's realized without it, we can't defend ourselves when the next Penelope or Lord Malfoy comes along." Lord Remy touched the sceptre gently with his forefinger. It lay still, quiet cold metal on black velvet.

"Now, Lily, how did you make the sceptre react." Lord Remy turned his gaze hopefully to Lucie.

"I touched it. Like this." Lucie leaned forward, touching the sceptre with her index finger. The sceptre responded with a tiny jolt of light, a tingling buzz of energy that raced up Lucie's finger sizzling through her arm. "That's when it reacts. It feels strange, like it's stinging me," she admitted to Lord Remy, vigorously shaking pins and needles from her hand.

"Amazing," Lord Remy murmured quietly to himself. "That would only happen if you had latent magic running in your blood. Another question, do you have any talents, any unusual abilities? Something we would consider a gift?"

"No." Lucie shook her head slowly. "That's why the sceptre's reaction confuses me."

"Any premonitions, have you ever seen something in the future?"

"No."

"Healing, communicating with animals, anything like that?" Lord Remy shoved his glasses up his nose.

"No." Lucie shook her head again.

"Hmm..." Remy's face fell. "I suppose I'll do some research. Fascinating this artifact responds to you like this. Especially with you being Lovanian." Lord Remy wrapped the velvet over the sceptre, concealing its glimmering surface beneath soft folds. "I'll get back to you when I have something." Lord Remy turned, ignoring Lucie to shuffle through a stack of papers, a few loose sheets flying from the pile and drifting to the dusty floor.

Lucie, realizing Lord Remy had dismissed her, let herself out the door, giving out a startled yelp, when she bumped into Frederich, hovering outside the office.

"Well?" Frederich asked anxiously as Lucie emerged.

"I still don't know why the sceptre keeps reacting to me," Lucie explained, brushing a streak of dust off her dress and sneezing.

"Don't worry. At least the sceptre is in our possession and not Penelope's. She can't access full power without it." Frederich reached up, brushing a tumbling lock of dark hair over Lucie's shoulder. "Come walk with me in the garden. I have a free hour; there's something I want to speak to you about." He swallowed nervously.

Apprehension clenched icy fingers around Lucie's heart when she saw the serious look on Frederich's face. Almost shy. She followed him outside, eyeing a book or two longingly as they wove through the dusty stacks. If she were here longer, she would definitely come back to investigate. Lucie trailed a finger down the spine of a particularly enticing-looking volume of fairy tales.

"Take the book with you," Frederick urged, noting Lucie's interest.

"Really?" Lucie pulled the book from the shelf, holding it tight against her chest.

"Sure, bring the book back when you're finished reading it. In fact, come any time for more books, Marthe keeps an extra library key somewhere. No one uses the library. Come and go whenever you please. There're chairs and a fireplace by that window." He pointed through a narrow passage toward a cozy sitting area.

Clutching her book, Lucie followed Frederick through the winding corridors of the castle, eventually arriving at the private rose garden. Frederich chose the path that curved around the lily pond. The scenery was pleasant. Queen Isabella's bright flowers splashed the area, attracting swarms of butterflies and perfuming the air with their scent. Frederich led Lucie to a wrought-iron bench, gesturing for her to sit next to him. Lucie arranged her skirt carefully, too nervous to admire the beautiful setting. The troubled look on Frederich's face made her stomach queasy. Her pulse pounded underneath her skin.

Frederich reached out a hand to touch her arm, then thought better of it, shoving it in his pocket instead. "I need to talk you about..."

"About?" Lucie looked down at her hands, white-knuckled around her book.

"Well... about us." Frederich swallowed, this throat bobbing.

The butterflies in Lucie's stomach echoed the ones in the garden, fluttering tumultuously. "Us?"

Just then, Celine's bubbly voice rang out, interrupting from behind an arrangement of rosebushes.

"There you are!" Celine bounded over, golden hair flying, seemingly oblivious to the intense conversation taking place.

"Mother said we can go for a ride and picnic at the lake today. Will you be two joining us?" Celine beamed sunnily. "Oh, sorry, am I interrupting something?" She looked from one face to another, noticing the tense atmosphere.

"No, no, it's fine." Lucie stood, brushing invisible grass from her skirt.

"Good, I wanted to show you the stables, one of my favourites just foaled." Celine linked arms with Lucie, dragging her down the path at a rapid clip ahead of Frederich. They followed the stone path through tall green hedges.

"What are you doing?" Celine whispered furiously after checking behind her, making sure Frederich was out of earshot. "At least flirt with Frederich a little, throw the poor man bone.

He's terrible with women; Mother says because he's never had to try before."

"I don't know how to flirt." Lucie sighed, wishing she had paid just a bit more attention to the tricks Blanchette used to get boys' attention back in Annecy.

"It's easy. Just stare into his eyes a lot and smile. Pretend everything he says is really interesting or funny depending on the situation." Celine instructed. "Oh, and if you get the chance, flip your hair. Like this." She demonstrated by tossing her silky blonde waterfall.

"Look, we're having a big party tonight, a ball to formally announce Frederich's return. I'll help you get ready. You'll be so beautiful that you won't have to make an effort after one look at you. I mean, Frederich's obviously crazy about you. He just needs that little something to give him a nudge." Celine gave Lucie a saucy wink.

"But—I'm not from nobility. I have nothing to offer Frederich. Not even a little," Lucie protested, flustered. "Frederich should at least make political connections, another alliance."

"Oh—that." Celine sniffed. "I'm pretty sure Mother and Father are convinced that's not the best course of action anymore." She leaned in close, whispering, "I overheard them talking about you and Frederich last night. Since everything happened with Penelope, they're allowing him to make his own choice about marriage. It's a good idea. After all, it benefits me too. if Frederich chooses who to marry, then I choose who to marry." Celine squeezed Lucie's arm. "Now come on, I actually *do* want to show you this horse." Leaving Frederich with growing frustration sweeping across his face, Celine swept Lucie down the path toward the stables.

CHAPTER TWENTY-SIX

Lucie surveyed her reflection in the vanity mirror.

She had to admit, Celine had done an amazing job dressing her. Borrowed jewels sparkled at Lucie's slender throat and wrists. The dress fit perfectly, thanks to the team of seamstresses sent to work under Celine and Katherine's eagle eye. The silk glided over her skin, gently kissing her curves with its softness.

Best of all was that afternoon when a knock sounded at the door. Lucie opened it, expecting another delivery, only to reveal a young woman with soft brown eyes and flowing copper curls. At first, Lucie was confused, but as soon as she heard the familiar lilt, she realized it was Fleur.

"Celine sent me to do your hair," Fleur's musical voice with its old-fashioned accent brought a welcome familiarity amid the strangeness of court. "If you'll have me?" a hesitant look entered the warm brown eyes.

"Of course." It was delightful to be reunited with her old friend, who had quickly made the castle her home.

When Lucie finally went downstairs, her nerves jangled; the flurry of activity surrounding her gave her the impression she was the centre attraction that evening. Lucie peeked inside the ballroom, sucking in a sharp breath when she saw the crowd gathering. Cold sweat gathered at the small of Lucie's back as whispering heads turned. Nervous, she scanned the room, hoping to see a familiar face; it was then she saw him. Across the expansive space, leaning on a tall column, chatting to an older gentleman, was Frederich. A wide smile lit up Frederich's face when he spotted Lucie, and he gestured for her to come. Swallowing hard, Lucie pushed her way through the throng, courage strengthened by the welcoming expression warming Frederich's eyes.

His smile widened as she glided closer. "You look beautiful."

Lucie blushed. "Thank you." She swished her skirt. "It was your sister's doing."

Frederich cleared his throat, a muscle in his jaw twitching, "Can I get you refreshments?" he waved toward a table laden with cool drinks and plates of food.

"No, thank you. I'm terrified of ruining my dress," Lucie admitted, fingering at the silk fabric of her gown.

"How about a dance?" Frederich offered his hand.

As Frederich's hand engulfed hers, Lucie was eternally grateful for the many hours of dance lessons Marion had forced on her. She followed confidently to the marble floor.

"This is the first time we've talked since we returned to Corvan." Frederich's arms were warm around Lucie as they spun and dipped, manoeuvring through a sea of colourful silk dresses.

"There's something I wanted to ask you." Frederich steered Lucie toward a gazebo looking into the ballroom. The night air, scented with roses and lilies from the garden, fanned Lucie's hot cheeks. It was quiet, only a few scattered lanterns broke the velvet darkness. Frederick leaned against the railing, drawing Lucie close, tucking her securely under his arm.

"Celine and I used to sneak into this gazebo and watch when we were too young to attend balls," he explained, reaching down to touch one of the dark curls that framed her face. "No one's ever discovered that entryway behind the pillar."

Lucie smiled, picturing two small golden-haired children peeking at a glamourous crowd of partygoers.

"Did you ever get caught?" her eyes were luminous in the reflected light.

"No, but I suspect everyone knew we were here." Frederich cleared his throat. "But that's why I brought you here." Frederich's voice hitched. "I want to—no, I *need* to tell you how I feel."

Every nerve ending tingled as her eyes met his. "How you feel?" Her voice was a mere whisper.

"I love you." He took her hand in his, thumb gently stroking her smooth skin. "... I have for a while. I'll understand if you don't..."

Lucie felt as though her heart would burst from her chest with joy and relief. "You do?"

"I do. You're unlike anyone I've ever met, and I can't imagine a life without you in it." He searched her eyes, looking for answers.

"I feel the same way." Lucie laughed softly at his sigh of relief.

"Even when I was—"

"Even then," Lucie interrupted him. "How could I not feel that way? You're so good, kind, and loyal."

Frederich wrapped Lucie in a fierce hug. "I can't wait to tell everyone." Frederich's voice caught with emotion. "Mother and Father will be delighted. And Celine, of course." He drew back and lowered his head to Lucie's upturned face for a gentle kiss.

Lucie's face, beaming with joy, gave the secret away as Frederich led her back into the ballroom. Frederich led her straight to the dais, where King Erich and Queen Isabella sat watching the festivities. Not letting go of Lucie's hand for an instant, Frederich lowered his head, whispering to King Erich. King Erich listened intently, letting out a tremendous laugh. Even Queen Isabella lit up with pleasure, squeezing Lucie's hand.

"We're delighted." Queen Isabella beamed.

"When can we make the announcement?" King Erich asked, not wanting to waste a moment.

"Well—I'd like to inform my family first if that's all right?" Lucie asked.

"Of course, dear," said Queen Isabella, "Very sensible. Although I believe they might already have an idea." Queen Isabella glanced pointedly across the room to where Pierre stood talking to one of the nobles, discussing trade, no doubt. His eyes met Frederich's briefly, a nod of understanding passing between them.

"I knew it." Celine barrelled into Lucie, swooping in with a flurry of lilac silk. Lucie turned from her sisters to embrace the younger girl, who was brimming with exhilaration. "I've always wanted a sister. Now I have three." Celine grinned at the three girls, blue eyes sparkling. The girls laughed.

Lucie, surrounded by the people she loved, felt as though she might explode from sheer happiness.

CHAPTER TWENTY-SEVEN

"Try one more time," Lord Remy encouraged Lucie, glasses sliding down his nose, cravat rumpled and askew.

Lucie narrowed her eyes obediently, focusing her energy on the unlit candle on the desk in front of her. Holding the sceptre tight, she concentrated all thoughts on imagining a lit flame on its wick. At this point, Lucie would settle for a tiny spark. She waited. Nothing happened, just cold dead air. She sighed, toying with the sceptre. Lucie could feel the energy from the sceptre, that tingle travelling up her arm, swarming through her body, setting every nerve ending alight. But when Lucie tried to take the sceptre's energy and use it, everything muddled and fizzled out. It slithered out from under her, sliding away like water.

Frustrated, Lucie rubbed the back of her neck with her free hand, pushing back a stray curl. She'd been practicing in Lord Remy's study all morning, and they had made no progress. It wasn't Lord Remy's fault. Lord Remy knew a lot *about* magic and appreciated the history of magic. But he didn't seem to know how to use it. Lord Remy gathered most of his information from dusty books that escaped the purge after the royal family banned magic, along with sparse details picked up traveling. Which, Lucie quickly discovered, meant there was precious little practical information.

"I might need to do a *smidge* of extra research," Lord Remy muttered, flicking through another dusty book. Lucie sat patiently as he licked his pudgy finger, flipping another page. "Ah yes, here."

Lord Remy turned to Lucie. "Water magic." He searched the desk, producing half a glass of brackish water. "This will do. Now, Leila, think about the water. Do you feel anything? Maybe a tingle?" he searched her face anxiously, spectacles sliding down his nose.

Lucie held the sceptre. "Yes, but there's always a tingle when I'm touching the sceptre." She complained, "It's not changing with the water."

"Hmm..." Lord Remy pulled his ear thoughtfully. "Discovering your gift would be much easier if we could find someone who practices magic regularly. Someone from Lovan ideally, but Iasia, Luixe—even the Islands would work. I know mages from the university in Florin, friends from my studies there, amazing what they do, but it would take weeks to bring them here." Lord Remy scratched his head, nearly knocking off his spectacles. "Are you sure you can't make the water react? Maybe make it ripple... bubble?"

"Wait a minute, my father might know a mage," Lucie supplied helpfully. "He travelled up and down the Iasian trade route with caravans. You know how traders gossip; he's surely heard something along the route. Of course, we would have to guarantee their safety." She gave Ruben a penetrating look.

Lord Remy's eyes flickered in thought, then lit up. "Wonderful. If you find a mage, I'll speak privately to King Erich. I think we definitely could arrange their safety."

Lord Remy didn't waste time. He immediately sent a steward scurrying; moments later, the steward returned with Pierre and offered him a comfortable seat in one of Lord Remy's overstuffed chairs, tea and pastries at his elbow.

"Lucie inherited magic from her mother, Avella's side." Pierre shot Lucie a guilty look. "I never told Lucie—Annecy is a small town. It would cause too much trouble; gossip. Avella's family was Iasian. We met when I was travelling with the caravan for trade. Her family was nobility, very aware of their position, preparing their daughters for life in court. When I met Avella, they wouldn't have anything to do with me. I was only a merchant, after all. Things got so bad between us we had to escape to Annecy. Avella's grandmother was a mighty mage; and bitter and angry with me. Avella's magic was sealed; we kept the secret and never discussed it. I think Avella was trying to protect me. She knew the dangers of practicing magic in Lovan."

"What kind of mage was mother?" Lucie leaned forward, drinking in Pierre's every word.

"Fire magic. And..." here, Pierre paused, lowering his voice, "Avella possessed a *book*."

"A book?" Lucie asked, wondering what the significance of the book was. Pierre kept a number of books in the library, tedious history books, boring ledgers, files of accounts, but Lucie didn't remember a book connected explicitly to her mother.

"Yes. Not a big book—this size." Anton gestured with his hands. "Full of strange writing, scripts, and symbols. The book was from her grandmother and was ancient and powerful. Very powerful. I carried the book with me. Even when I lost the business, and we lost everything else, I always had it in my pocket to keep it safe." He lowered his voice. "If anyone recognized the book, we would have been in terrible danger."

"Do you still have the book?" Lucie worried her lip anxiously. Her eyes darted to Pierre's pocket.

Pierre shook his head sadly. "No, unfortunately, the fire destroyed the book."

Lord Remy, who had hardly dared breathe out excitement during Pierre's speech, slumped back in his chair. Suddenly, he perked up as a thought occurred to him. "Would you recognize the book; if you saw the writing or symbols or something similar?"

Pierre nodded. "Definitely. I'd know those symbols in my sleep."

"Follow me." Lord Remy put a finger on his lips, beckoning to Lucie and her father, leading them to a dusty, forgotten corner of the library. After checking carefully to make sure they were alone, Lord Remy moved a stack of books leaning precariously against an ancient tapestry. He pulled the tapestry aside, revealing a small wooden door with an old-fashioned iron lock.

"Wait, a minute." Lord Remy patted his pockets, finally drawing out a small key. The cupboard creaked open. Lucie peeked inside; a shelf groaned under a large stack of ancient manuscripts, some so dog-eared Lucie wondered if anyone could read them at all.

"Achoo." Lord Remy sneezed, reaching in to lift a stack out. "Do any of these books look familiar?"

Pierre took one, wiping a thick layer of dust off the top cover before opening it. "Nothing like this one." He thumbed cautiously through the brittle pages, scrutinizing the symbols. One by one, Pierre examined each book. Replacing each volume until he reached two-thirds of the way through the stack. A disappointed look swept across Lord Remy's face, growing as Pierre set each book aside.

"This one." Pierre held up a slim volume, its brown cover cracked with age. He carefully passed it to Lord Remy, who in turn handed it to Lucie.

"Should I open it?" Hesitation slid across her face. Apprehension slithered up her spine as she gingerly held the small volume.

Lord Remy nodded. Slowly, very slowly, Lucie turned the first page. Spidery writing scrawled across the parchment. As she stared at the letters, Lucie's vision blurred. Gradually the letters formed words. Words Lucie could read. She glanced up, wondering if she should continue. Lord Remy nodded encouragingly. She cleared her throat and began reading. Immediately the sceptre responded, flaring to life, sending a bolt of heat and light shooting across the room. A pile of papers across the room crackled into flames. After he doused the papers with a glass of water, reducing them to a smouldering mess, Lord Remy sat down, breathing heavily.

"You're going to need another tutor." Lord Remy absently rubbed the gold ring on his finger. "I'm going to need someone who actually *practices* magic to guide Lucie if we're going to continue. It would be too dangerous for everyone involved if I try to train Lucie myself. I'm really more of a... collector."

"Well," Pierre hesitated, "Althea knows magic. She's always had a soft spot for Lucie. I think if you ensured discretion, she might agree to help us."

"Althea?" Lord Remy tilted his head.

"The herb-woman in Annecy," Lucie said. "She's one of the best healers around. It wouldn't surprise me if Althea was gifted."

"How soon can we get Althea here?"

CHAPTER TWENTY-EIGHT

From the moment Althea arrived, Lucie's training began in earnest.

"Picture what you want to happen with your mind when you read the script." Lord Remy didn't want to take any more chances with his precious collection of books and manuscripts. So he assigned them to a large empty room located at the top of the west wing tower, far away from the bustling castle life, where their activities would remain discreet.

Lucie closed her eyes, conscious of the weight of two pairs of eyes boring into her, focusing her mind to the best of her ability. She concentrated on the small clay pot Althea had placed on the wooden desk in front of her, three seeds nestled into the rich, damp soil it contained. She opened her eyes, staring at the page of strange, slanted writing scrawling... swarming across the pages. Once again, swirling texts danced in front of Lucie's eyes, shaping into words. After Lucie read the words out loud, Althea dug a gnarled finger in the flowerpot, gently stirring the soil to reveal the seeds; protective outer shells winking from her wrinkled hand. Nothing. Lucie leaned her head against the chair. Frustration sweeping through her. Did she really even have a gift?

"It might take time to find the gift suited to you." Althea laid a comforting hand on Lucie's dark hair. "Here, let's try this page. It's for changing the form of an object. It's mostly used with water to change it to ice or steam."

"Oh, that is good." Lord Remy's eyes gleamed from an overstuffed armchair. His short legs hovered over the floor. "We fought ancient battles using ice weapons. And even now, there's a powerful ice princess in a northern kingdom. Ice would be a wonderful gift. Wonderful." He shoved his glasses back onto the bridge of his nose, but they slipped down again immediately.

Althea placed a bowl of water in front of Lucie. "Here you are, dear. Take all the time you need." Lucie inhaled deeply, drawing her shoulders back in determination. Focusing her energy on the script racing across the parchment while staring hard at the bowl of water. The water lay smooth and still in the bowl, not even a shiver of movement rippling its smooth surface.

"Should we start at the beginning again?" Hours had passed, and even cheery Lord Remy drooped with exhaustion.

Lucie paged to the beginning of the book. Fire. Such a destructive, useless gift, she thought, watching Althea balance a pile of tinder in the fireplace. Again, Lucie closed her eyes, but she was tired. This time her concentration slipped. Bang. A jolt of energy so powerful it felt like it would tear her apart shot through Lucie's fingers. A deafening roar shook the room. The tinder crackled in a whirlwind of flames, shooting sparks in every direction, setting the rug on fire.

"Well, we know your gift works." Althea poured a pitcher of water onto the blazing rug, reducing it to a singed hole in the wool. Lord Remy clapped his hands with delight.

"Wonderful, just wonderful." His eyes twinkled at Lucie. "Much more powerful than yesterday. I think we're definitely onto something now."

"I did that?" Lucie stared in dismay at the mess she had caused. "It's so destructive, can't we keep trying, just to see if there's anything else? Another gift?"

"Of course we can, dear," Althea said. "There's still a lot to try, but remember, it's unusual for anyone to have more than one gift. If fire is your gift, you'll be happiest if you accept it. All gifts can be good if they follow pure intentions."

Lucie's voice was small. She glanced again at the smoking hole in the priceless rug. "Yes, let's definitely keep trying."

They spent the rest of the afternoon poring through the book, trying every avenue. Failing all of them. Nothing else worked, not healing, not foreshadowing, not communicating with animals, although Lucie enjoyed stroking the fluffy kitten Althea brought from the stables. Not even poison. Just fire, and if that wasn't awful enough, the fire became more potent every time Lucie used her gift.

"I think we've tried all the known gifts." Althea finally sat back in her chair, sipping from a cooling cup of tea.

Lucie rubbed a hand across her exhausted face. "So now what?"

"Now, you become the best fire mage you can be. That is if you're willing." Althea frowned at the tea, setting the cup down.

"All right." Lucie pressed her lips together. "I'll learn to make fire."

"But not tonight." Althea continued. "These old bones need a rest." She smiled, gesturing out the window toward the fading light of the sun. "First, have a good night's sleep. I've made tea that will help you feel stronger, more focused. We'll start first thing light in the morning."

CHAPTER TWENTY-NINE

Lucie dreamed of fire.

Torches wielded by angry villagers, destroying her cabin. Flames burning the caravans to blackened carcasses, destroying lives and livelihoods. Embers Lucie herself created with nothing but her mind and blood.

At dawn, Lucie rose, dressing simply in a tunic and breeches, pulling on long leather boots, slipping through grey morning light straight to the arena. Celine would be there; she practiced without fail early mornings. Lucie crept inside quietly, watching the girl glide through her paces, flying through the air with grace and strength. When Celine finally halted in front of her, panting heavily with exertion, Lucie handed her a cloth.

"How do you do it?" she asked as Celine sat next to her, skin glowing from hard work.

"Do what?" Celine gratefully took the cloth, mopping beads of sweat from her face.

"Practice a skill that kills—destroys. I saw your state after you killed the mage in the forest. It tortured you. Yet you're determined to come to the arena without fail, practicing every morning. Why?"

Lucie searched Celine's face. Hoping—praying for answers. Real answers.

Celine paused, pleating the cloth into a tiny square. "You're right, fighting is terribly destructive, but I believe it's necessary. I use my skills to protect myself and the people I love." The words were simple, but truth pierced Lucie straight to the heart.

After breakfast, Lucie sent word for Althea and met the elderly woman in the arena.

"Let's get started. Teach me how to be a fire mage." Lucie's eyes were narrowed, her face set. If this was her gift, she would make the best of it.

From that moment, Lucie's days were hectic. Rising early every morning, practicing with Celine before sessions under Althea's tutelage. After that, lunch with Queen Isabella, under whose wing she learned the inner workings of court life and politics. Even with, or perhaps because of her busy schedule, Lucie heard rumbles and snatches of gossip about unrest boiling in Iasia.

After her altercation with Lucie and Frederich, Queen Penelope had never reappeared. Word was filtering across the Lovanian border that the Iasian throne lay empty. The Duke ruled temporarily in her absence. But because Penelope was officially alive, the Duke had little power; making actual decisions or creating change was impossible. The Iasians, already miserable from years of extortionate taxes and excess labour were protesting. And Iasia wasn't the only troubled kingdom.

Whispers of Lucie's magic had permeated the kingdom of Lovan. After hundreds of years of magic ban, people viewed this development with extreme suspicion; accusations of witchcraft and sorcery spread like wildfire. It delighted others. Even after the purge and subsequent prohibition, pockets of magic survived. Because of Lucie's boldness, a handful of magic users plucked up enough courage to emerge from hiding, seeking refuge and safety within the castle walls. A move not well received by the general population. Lucie's heart broke to hear the stories of people hunted and persecuted for magic, but it only fueled her determination to work harder.

"Well done." Althea smiled in approval, gripping her cane with gnarled fingers.

After weeks of practice, Lucie's ability to control magic improved in leaps and bounds. She could now hone her fire to the point where she could gently warm a cup of tea and aim with such ease and precision that the barest flick of her finger could direct it. The book was no longer needed. Lucie memorized the foreign script and only had to close her eyes and recall the words on the page to access her powers. Lucie hadn't tested the upper limits of her powers, but she and Althea both suspected it was significantly stronger than they first assumed. After Lucie exploded a giant fir tree on the outskirts of the castle garden and nearly set the castle wall on fire, she had stuck to smaller refinements of her skill.

"Fantastic," Frederich shouted from the sidelines, applauding. He enjoyed watching Lucie practice whenever he could get away from political duties.

Lucie smiled. She had used her index finger to shoot thread-like points of fire at three small targets set across the grassy field. "Thank you." She used a bucket of water to douse the flames before plopping next to Frederich on the grass.

"My mother said to ask if you prefer lilies or roses." Frederick dropped a kiss on Lucie's nose.

Lucie chewed her lip thoughtfully. "I don't know.... I like all flowers. Do I *have* to choose?"

"Both then." Frederich decided. "And what about colour?"

"Pink, I guess?" Queen Isabella and her staff had inundated Lucie with wedding details once they announced the engagement. The sheer number of decisions to make had overwhelmed her since.

"And you have another dress fitting. At three. Katherine insisted you be on time for this one."

Lucie rolled her eyes, "I've had enough fittings for twenty dresses now." she complained. Katherine had thrown herself enthusiastically into Lucie's wedding plans, becoming thick as thieves with Queen Isabella, chatting over silks and jacquards and different shades of lace.

"Has Katherine returned from Annecy?" Lucie took the hand Frederich offered to stand, brushing grass from her tunic.

"I saw her at breakfast this morning. She said Mary is going to start weaving fabric for her and Marion's dresses."

"Really?" Lucie began collecting targets. Althea had left, insisting she needed rest, but judging from the sly expression on her face, Lucie assumed it was a ploy to give her and Frederich some much-needed time alone.

"I'm surprised Mary came around so quickly. People in Annecy were so—agitated—although it helped when we sent people to repair Annecy town hall for them." Lucie shuddered. She had no desire to return to Annecy after the fire and subsequent events. Even under King Erich's protection.

"The Annecian's are the ones who should apologize to you. Don't think I'm going to let their behaviour go that easy." Frederich's face was grim. "I saw how they acted like a pack of wild animals."

"People act like that when they're scared." Lucie dismissed his concerns with a wave of her hand. "At least Mary is being reasonable now. She took Katherine in and cared for her when all that awful business happened with Father—they were such dear friends. The others will come around, eventually. Henri and Izzie are sensible, and people listen to them. If it weren't for Blanchette's tricks and gossip, they wouldn't have turned against me in the beginning. The truth will come out." Lucie swallowed, determinedly pushing back feelings of loss and regret. It stung that Annecy had so easily turned its back on her. The pair strolled across the meadow toward the castle, Frederich lugging targets and Lucie carrying the empty bucket.

As they neared the outer courtyard, Celine met them, dashing breathlessly across the courtyard to meet them, "Come quick. Someone's spotted a fleet of ships sailing into harbour; it's huge." She doubled over, panting with exertion.

CHAPTER THIRTY

"The fleet is too distant to identify flags or insignia, but they counted forty ships; maybe more. Iasian built from what I've heard. Everyone knows they've been building *trade* ships. Father's calling an emergency council meeting right now." Celine raised her eyebrows, lowering her voice, as she emphasized the word trade.

"Aren't there always ships sailing into harbour?" Lucie asked as they jogged briskly for the council room at a rapid clip. "The harbour is busy, especially now. There're no storms this season. It's when Father conducted most of his business."

"Yes, but it's extremely rare for an entire fleet to come in together without warning—especially an unknown fleet. The harbour master didn't recognise these ships." Celine panted.

The fact that only half the council was present didn't prevent a lively discussion from ensuing. The others barely noticed Lucie and Frederich as they slid breathlessly into their seats at the polished table.

"We must go immediately. With the biggest army we can muster." Lord Gunther lowered his bushy eyebrows into a fierce expression, glowering. "Everyone knows Iasia has been plotting—planning something. After what happened to Frederich, we shouldn't take any chances. This is clearly an act of war."

235

"It may just be a delegation from the Ronain Islands." Queen Isabella spoke in a reasonable tone. "If we're too aggressive, it'll cause more trouble. Trouble Lovan can't afford. People are already in an uproar because we lifted the magic ban. If we cause more turmoil, there will be pandemonium."

Several council members, including Lord Remy, nodded sagely in agreement at this suggestion.

"That's exactly why we should send the army. If we're seen passively doing nothing, there might be *more* of an uproar." Lord Gunther clenched his meaty fist. "These ships are an obvious threat to our kingdom."

A sharp knock interrupted the escalating dispute. "Pardon, Your Majesty. The harbour master is here requesting an audience. He says it's vitally important."

"Send him in." King Erich's deep voice rumbled from the head of the table.

The harbour master, smelling of salt, fish, and sea, stood before the council, worried expression creasing his weathered face.

"It's the ships." He twisted his cap nervously in his hands. "There's something strange about the ships. They aren't—natural."

"What do you mean the ships aren't natural?" Lord Gunther's voice broke through the stunned silence following the harbour master's announcement.

"Well, that's why I thought I should come to explain myself." The harbour master met the council with steady eyes. "The ships are sailing against the wind; their sails aren't furled. It's like they're self-powered. It's impossible, unheard of. And I've been working at that harbour for near fifty years now. And the ship's speed is unusual too. They're coming in fast. Faster than any known ship can sail."

Stunned silence settled across the table. Penelope.

"When do you expect the ships to arrive?" A frown gave away Queen Isabella's apprehension.

"They'll be here by mid-afternoon.... two hours, I reckon. There are forty-five ships." The harbour master shifted his feet. He looked terrified, face pale under the deep-lined tan.

"Are the ships close enough for us to see flags? Or emblems?" King Erich asked.

"That's the other strange thing. They have a flag, but it's one I don't recognize. No one's seen it before. A purple background with a red dragon."

Lucie and Frederich exchanged looks. "We've seen that emblem. Penelope used it as her personal coat of arms."

At this news, a series of worried glances circled the room. This wasn't much warning. The harbour was a half-hour away by horseback. And they had to gather the soldiers.

"Send all soldiers from the castle." King Erich spoke decisively. "And send messengers to the nearest outposts to secure help." He gestured to his aide, who scurried off to do his bidding.

Soon the castle was in a state of tumult as King Erich's soldiers scrambled to prepare to meet the ships.

"Should I go with the soldiers?" Lucie spoke in a hushed voice to Prince Frederich as she surveyed the soldiers marching out of the castle gates. "I could use fire to help."

"No," Frederich swung into the saddle. "Far too dangerous. We don't know if they're armed or if they intend to fight. Let us assess the situation first. We might need your fire later." He leaned down, pressing a kiss to Lucie's upturned lips before joining Lord Gunther and the others, clattering through the winding streets of Corvan.

CHAPTER THIRTY-ONE

Lucie paced the library, pausing to stare out the window. She came with Katherine, hoping to lose herself in a book. Goodness knows there was precious little time for leisure the past week. But she couldn't concentrate. Lucie threw herself into a deep leather armchair next to Katherine, who was busy sewing a concoction of lace and silk, frothy waves spilling across her lap.

"It's likely traders from far away. You know a fleet arrives occasionally." Katherine bit off the end of her thread and examined her work, a hint of satisfaction playing around her lips. "You know, they just can't be too careful with everything else that's happening. They'll be some explanation, don't worry." She carefully licked her index finger, choosing a strand of blue thread.

"I know." Lucie flicked through a book, scanning the pages haphazardly. "I have a terrible feeling that something isn't *right*." The feeling had only strengthened since Frederich and the army left for the coast. Pulsing deep in Lucie's chest, stifling her with its thick presence.

A rattle at the window pulled Lucie's attention away from her book. "What was that?" Lucie's head jerked up, eyes searching the windows. Only blue sky, dotted with fluffy white clouds, met her eyes.

"Probably one of those birds Queen Isabella keeps in the garden. One perched on my windowsill yesterday, staring at me for hours." Unfazed, Katherine re-threaded her needle and continued to sew. Tossing aside the book she was fidgeting with, Lucie went over to the window, working the stiff latch until the window swung open with a loud screech. She stuck her head out, peering around the small garden that surrounded the library.

"I don't see anything-—oh!"

A swirling grey cloud seeped through the open window, a mass hovering a few inches over the floor. Lucie stared, mouth open as the writhing form shifted and twisted, gradually solidifying, taking the shape of a woman. A chillingly beautiful, familiar woman.

"Penelope?" gasped Lucie, frozen feet refusing to move from their spot on the floor.

The distorted shape came into focus with a shiver. Penelope stepped forward, beautiful face marred by fury.

"You thought you'd swoop in and take my place, did you?" Penelope strode menacingly toward Lucie.

"No," Lucie protested, legs wobbling like jelly. "It wasn't like that." she straightened, holding her hand in front of her, willing her fire. It shot out, a golden stream, cutting through the air like a knife.

"Well, it certainly *looks* like that's what happened. This is *my* throne." Penelope smirked, waving her fingers in the air; the fire bounced off her, sizzling into limp strands of steam.

With lightning speed, Penelope shot forward, putting icy hands around Lucie's neck, squeezing with steely strength. Lucie kicked, catching the other girl's shin with her boot, and

Penelope yelped, sparks of anger shooting from her eyes, but her hands didn't slip even when Lucie clawed them, fighting to drag them away. Just when black spots were swimming before Lucie's eyes, she felt the grip loosen. Penelope yelled in pain, clutching her side. Blood spilled over her fingers.

Lucie glanced up. Katherine stood, heaving, holding her scissors. With a feral cry, Penelope sprang at Katherine, grappling her to the floor.

This was her chance. If she had the sceptre, she could fight back. Destroy Penelope once and for all. Woozy, Lucie scrambled to her feet, stumbling toward Lord Remy's office.

Behind her, Katherine and Penelope engaged in a vicious struggle. Penelope howled, furious as Katherine grabbed a handful of long hair, yanking hard. Lucie scrabbled at the office door, praying desperately it wasn't locked. Success. The handle turned; she squinted against the sudden darkness of the small room. Fumbling, Lucie frantically tried to remember the last time she had seen the sceptre, hurriedly rifling through stacks of papers on the enormous desk, knocking a teetering pile of books to the ground with a loud crash.

In the next room, the fight between Katherine and Penelope grew more violent. Just when Lucie thought she'd never find the sceptre, she bumped into something hard wrapped in velvet. There it was. She ripped away the velvet covering, snatching up the heavy metal sceptre. Spinning, she ran to where Katherine and Penelope still struggled.

If Lucie could separate Katherine and Penelope enough strike, she would have a chance to defeat Penelope. Lucie shouted, pointing the sceptre at Penelope, hoping the sight would distract Penelope long enough for Katherine to escape.

Sparks shot out, crackling in the air. Penelope jerked her head, eyes glazed with fury as she caught sight of the sceptre. She wrapped Katherine in a headlock with an angry howl, using her as a shield to block Lucie's aim. Narrowing her eyes, Penelope reached into her pocket, pulling out another sceptre. It was nearly identical to Lucie's, but instead of colourful gems, this sceptre was encrusted with a gleaming layer of blue-white stones. Penelope shoved Katherine into a crumpled heap on the floor; her sceptre glowed with fierce white light. Penelope raised her arm, pointing the sceptre directly at Lucie. Lucie flung up her own sceptre, barely blocking the stream of icy particles shooting out. Her hand shook with the effort. She heard blood pounding in her ears, the sizzle of magic thick over and under her skin.

Dread curled icy fingers in Lucie's stomach; she realized she had to act fast or risk setting the library and possibly the entire castle on fire. Gritting her teeth, Lucie felt the power streaming through her body, shooting through her sceptre. With a loud cry, Penelope blocked it; the two girls spent the next few moments locked in a deadly skirmish, Lucie working intently to steer Penelope toward the window where she could unleash her full power. Penelope, catching onto her plan, danced away, her movements a mere blur.

It's now or never, thought Lucie, her energy flagging. She aimed the sceptre at Penelope and missed, smashing the tall window behind Penelope. Broken glass showered down, shards gleaming like diamonds. Instantly, Penelope was behind Lucie, grabbing her arm, wrenching it up sharply. Pain shot up Lucie's arm as she crashed to her knees. Penelope dove on top of her, holding her sceptre to Lucie's neck.

"No one takes what's mine," Penelope hissed, yanking viciously on Lucie's injured arm. Lucie's vision blurred with agony. She was about to faint. Reaching deep, she used the last of her strength, turned her head, and bit Penelope as hard as she could. Penelope shrieked in surprise, and Lucie closed her eyes, putting everything she had through her sceptre and into Penelope.

Screaming in rage, Penelope fell, the sceptre sliding from her fingers and rolling across the floor. A hideous stench burned through Lucie's nostrils, and she backed away, stomach churning with revulsion. A wisp of foul-smelling smoke curled from Penelope's motionless form, face frozen in one last vengeful expression of surprise. Pushing down her nausea, Lucie staggered toward Katherine, who groaned, rubbing a large goose egg on her forehead.

The door burst open. Frederich, face distorted in shock, took in the grotesque scene before him.

"Lucie! What happened?" Frederich knelt beside her, throwing his arms around her.

"Penelope." Queasy and exhausted, Lucie rested her head against Frederich's shoulder. It was over.

"When we reached the harbour, the seas were empty. I knew instantly Penelope used the ships as a distraction to lure Father's army away. An illusion. A good one, Penelope must have accessed a source without the sceptre."

Lucie reached under the little table where the other sceptre had rolled. "She had this." The warm metal buzzed against Lucie's hand. Frederich reached out to touch the winking diamonds on the handle.

"It's another of the kingdom sceptres, see this crest?" he breathed, pointing to the pattern engraved in the sceptre's handle. "Penelope had another sceptre all along."

"We'll have to show Lord Remy and King Erich." Lucie set the sceptre on a side table, not wanting to touch it more than necessary.

That evening, after a hot bath and much-needed clean clothes, Lucie curled up in the lounge of the royal apartments. Fresh beeswax candles and overflowing vases of Peonies—Queen Isabella's favourite—scented the air. Lucie leaned against the soft cushion and sipped from a cup of spiced cider.

"We'll send a delegation to Iasia immediately." King Erich spoke from his seat by the cracking fire. "The duke is sensible. He'll understand Lovan was defending against attack. Penelope's caused havoc in Iasia for a while. Hopefully, Duke Ruben will be a wonderful change for Iasia. We'll return the Iasian royal sceptre with the delegation."

"What about the other sceptre?" Lucie glanced at the shining object, gleaming softly from its resting place next to her elbow.

"I doubt the Iasians knew she had the Lovanian sceptre. We'll mention it, of course, but officially the sceptre belongs to Lovan, and since you're the only one who can use it, you, Lucie, will be the wielder."

"Me? but I'm just a commoner." Lucie reached out to touch the sceptre. It shimmered, sending a shiver of energy coursing up her arm. Magic tingled, drifting through the air.

"I think it's yours already." King Erich watched as the sceptre responded to Lucie's touch. "And you're not a commoner anymore. You're getting a title when you marry Prince Frederich. Princess Lucie."

LUCIE PAUSED IN THE hallway, peeking out the tall windows overlooking Corvan. Astonished that even this early—well before dawn—well-wishers crowded the castle gates. Unable to sleep, Lucie had taken a walk to calm her nerves. Excitement danced down her spine. This was the first time Lucie would officially meet the citizens—*her* citizens—she reminded herself. Letting herself back into the room, Fleur greeted her with an offering of fragrant, sticky sweet rolls for breakfast.

"You always know exactly what I need." Lucie sank to the cushioned seat at the vanity and allowed Fleur to comb her long hair, taming flyaway curls into a curtain of silk around her slim shoulders. The dizzying array of festivities started last week and gradually built to a fever pitch over the past two days. But today was the big day. The wedding day. Beginning with an early morning ceremony in the chapel followed by a wedding lunch, an appearance to the Lovanian citizens, and the finale—the wedding ball. Katherine was in her element organizing a multitude of fabulous dresses for Lucie to wear; Katherine's knowledge of fabrics and styles impressed even the royal wardrobe mistress, a fact Katherine enjoyed repeating to Lucie as frequently as possible.

Lucie slid into a gauzy dress, soft lace that clung to her slim figure drifting in undulating waves around her feet.

"Lovely, perfect." Fleur stood back, admiring Lucie. "Just one more thing." Fleur reached for a small embroidered pouch in the vanity drawer, spilling out the necklace Red had given Lucie back in the chateau.

"How were you able to save it?" Lucie let the gleaming chain slither through her fingers.

"It was in my pocket. I carried it to Corvan." Fleur fastened the necklace around Lucie's neck. "It somehow survived the chateau's destruction." She patted the clasp. "*Now* you're ready." Fleur smiled.

The wedding day flew by in a blur of activity. Lucie only remembered snatches of details. The look in Frederich's eyes as they stood in the quiet chapel surrounded by loved ones, colourful rose petals floating through the air as they ran through the cheering crowd. The villagers of Annecy cheering her on with the rest of the Lovanians and the proud looks on her father and sisters' faces. Happy and content at the end of the night, Lucie stood with Frederich, watching the fireworks display Queen Isabella organized for the close of the wedding evening.

"I can't believe it's over; are you sure you have to leave so soon?" Lucie asked her father, digging into an enormous plate of bacon and eggs. They were sitting in the breakfast room, the large open window letting in streaming sunshine along with the scent of freshly cut grass.

"I must meet the other guild leaders as soon as possible," Pierre said. "They can't think King Erich and Queen Isabella made me guild leader just because of my royal connections." he tweaked Lucie's nose. "Besides, I'll be back soon. We're only living down the street from you."

"I know. But everything's different now." Lucie took a large rasher of bacon from the platter, popping it in her mouth.

"A good different," Pierre answered. "You belong here. And people already love you, just give them time. Your sisters and I will be here whenever you need us." They turned their heads as a rap at the door interrupted them.

"Excuse me, Your Highness?" a castle aide stood at the door. "I know it's early, but there's someone here. They're insisting they need to speak to you personally." Lucie quirked a brow, wondering who would want to see her this early in the morning.

"Show them in."

To Lucie's surprise, Henri entered the room, twisting his old felt hat between large work-worn hands. Blanchette trailed unwillingly behind him, her usually snide expression subdued by the surrounding finery. Lucie's fork stopped halfway to her mouth. "Henri, Blanchette." She nodded at her former friends.

Henri spoke first, stammering. "It's just, I didn't want to interrupt you last night, being your wedding. But I wanted—no, I needed to tell you something important—I only discovered the truth last week."

"Discovered what?" Lucie swallowed the bacon and eyed the remaining pieces on the platter as she waited patiently for Henri to say his piece.

"Blanchette?" Henri nudged his daughter with a stern look.

"I'm sorry for what I did to you," Blanchette muttered, eyes glued to the pattern in the carpet.

"Sorry for what?" Lucie was torn between satisfaction at seeing Blanchette squirm after the suffering she caused and feeling pity for the girl who was clearly out of her element.

"Sorry for causing you trouble." Blanchette twisted her hands together in front of her.

Lucie decided to put the other girl out of her misery, at least for Henri's sake. "Don't worry about it. Everything worked out in the end." She waved at the empty seats graciously. "Would you like some breakfast? The bacon's delicious."

"Thank you." Henri cautiously perched at the edge of the brocade chair, looking nervously at the array of cutlery spread out in front of him.

"Coffee?" Lucie poured two cups of the hot, bitter liquid. "Blanchette, you take cream?" She added a generous dollop of cream to one of the cups, handing it to Blanchette.

"I never should have believed you could steal from me," Henri admitted, taking a sip of the coffee. "It wasn't until last week Blanchette finally told us everything."

"What *exactly* did Blanchette tell you?" Lucie and her father exchanged a glance, wondering how far Blanchette went in her quest for honesty.

"She told me someone set you up for stealing the silver."

"I see. And did Blanchette say *who* set me up?" Lucie gave Blanchette a pointed look.

"She told me she saw one of the soldiers do it." Henri set the cup down.

Lucie pressed her lips together, staring hard at Blanchette, "How would one of the soldiers do that? They left early that night. You know your father keeps the safe a secret and only counts the money after everyone leaves."

Henri swivelled his head toward his daughter, who had a mutinous expression on her pretty face.

"Well, maybe they came back after we closed the tavern." Blanchette shrugged, but a nervous twitch near her eye gave her away.

"And sneaked past the dog, through the locked door, with no one hearing or seeing?" Lucie challenged, not intending to let Blanchette get away with her lies this time. A defeated look crept over Blanchette's face as Lucie continued, a note of steel entering her voice. "Why don't you tell your father the truth. You took it because you were jealous. You wanted to see me in trouble. Even if it meant I would go hungry. And my sisters."

By now, Blanchette's cheeks were the shade of a ripe tomato. Henri turned on her, a rare angry expression crossing his kind face.

"Do you know what you've done? She's the crown princess now." He turned toward Lucie, pleading. "I hope you can find it in your heart to forgive us."

Lucie met his expression gravely. "You did hurt me at the time. But *you* did what you thought right. However," she nodded toward Blanchette, "any trouble out of you in the future and there will be consequences. I expect you to go tell everyone the truth. And I'll find out if you don't; Katherine and Marion intend to visit Annecy regularly." She gave the girl a piercing look.

Blanchette bowed her head in acknowledgement, a sullen look lurking in her eyes. "Now, you may go." Coffee forgotten, the pair scurried out, leaving Lucie to eat her breakfast in peace.

"Well done. It's high time someone put that girl in her place after everything she did to you." Frederich grinned, emerging from behind the door where he'd been hiding.

"Frederich. How much did you hear?" Lucie's cheeks flamed.

"Pretty much everything." Frederich grinned. "You did wonderfully—what's this? Did you eat all the bacon?" He looked at the bacon platter, which now only contained traces of grease. "The council is meeting today; I need a substantial breakfast to keep my strength up."

Lucie groaned, "I'm not looking forward to another three-hour council meeting. What is the subject this time?"

"The delegation we're sending to Iasia. Celine wants to go." Frederich scraped a heaping pile of eggs onto his plate.

"She does?" Lucie had to admit, she wasn't surprised. Celine was anxious to get more involved in everything.

"Yes, especially when she heard the duke has two sons." Frederich dug into a fresh platter of bacon that had been delivered.

"Do you think they'll let her go?" Lucie added a spoonful of honey to her coffee before tasting it.

Frederich shrugged. "I don't know. Things have calmed down in Iaisa from what we understand. We have so much work here, there's no way we'd be allowed to join the Iasian delegation—that reminds me—I have a meeting with Althea and Lord Remy today."

"About the mage guilds?"

"Yes, apparently there's incredible demand for healers; mage healers can do much more now they're allowed to practice openly. Every town is demanding a mage healer."

"That's good. At least people are accepting the healers. What about the other mage guilds?"

"Well—" Lucie hesitated. "It takes time for people to forget prejudices. I think it helps that they all know what happened between Penelope and me; they see the benefit of fire
magic. Some other guilds are proving useful as well. Accepting
magic isn't an overnight process."

"Have you needed to use the army to settle the citizens at
all?" Katherine asked, joining the table. King Erich had tasked
the army to protect fledgling guild members who frequently
faced enormous hostility from the general population.

"Not near the capital. Just the uprisings in the western
mountains the army put down—village riots—burnings. Once
we get the guilds established there, it should help settle things.
Father will use his trade connections to push the guilds. He
understands how the Iasian magic guilds work because of his
travels with the caravans. Lord Remy thinks I should still go
and see the Iasian guilds myself because I'm the patron." Lucie
stirred her coffee, sipping delicately.

Celine burst into the breakfast room, glowing and dishevelled from morning practice. "Oh good, we have toast left." She
slathered on butter and jam before taking a huge bite. "Father
says I can go to the council meeting today. Do you think that
means...?" Celine's voice trailed off hopefully.

"That he wants you to join the delegation? Maybe." Lucie
smiled at Celine's eager face.

After a tedious, long council meeting where the pros and
cons of whether Celine should join the delegation were discussed in excruciating detail, it was decided. Celine would join
the delegation to Iaisia. They spent the next few weeks in a flurry of preparation.

"I'm so excited." Celine swung into the saddle of her energetic-looking mount. Her sword gleamed proudly at her side.

"Remember what I told you about jumping into things without thinking first." King Erich reminded her as Celine waited impatiently for the contingent to be on their way. "And ride in the carriage if you're tired. It's a long trip."

"I'll be fine." Celine scoffed at the carriage, currently occupied by Sarah, her lady's maid. She twisted in her saddle, waving at the crowd of Lovanians gathered to see her off.

"And listen to Lord Gunther." Queen Isabella advised. "He has a lot of experience. Remember, we have to learn how mage guilds operate from Iasia, but Iasia needs our support as well. They have a world of damage to undo after Penelope, don't forget we have plenty to offer. Use your advantages."

"I will." Celine fidgeted with her reins. Her eyes wandered longingly toward the castle gates.

After more last-minute instructions, King Erich and Queen Isabella waved Celine off'; a cheer rising from the crowd as the delegation pranced through the castle gates down the Corvan streets. "I'm worried. Do you think Celine will be all right?" Queen Isabella's voice held a note of apprehension as she watched Celine's golden hair disappear around the last corner.

"Of course." King Erich's voice was confident, but more than a hint of concern lurked behind his eyes as he considered his well-intentioned but impulsive daughter.

Lucie squeezed Prince Frederich's arm as they turned back toward the castle. Whatever happened, Lucie knew Celine had far more strength and resilience than people gave her credit for. She was going to be just fine.

Find out what happens to Celine and Prince Alexander in Iasia. Read the next installment of the Crown and the Sceptre Series: **Strong: A Fairy Tale Retelling of the Princess and the Pea.**

Available for download now

Other Books by Kristina J Jordan

Free – A Fairy Tale Retelling of Rapunzel mybook.to/free[1]

Brave – A Fairy Tale Retelling of Beauty and the Beast mybook.to/bravekjj[2]

Strong – A Fairy Tale Retelling of the Princess and the Pea mybook.to/strongkjj[3]

True – A Fairy Tale Retelling of Puss in Boots mybook.to/True[4]

Loyal – A Fairy Tale Retelling of Red Riding Hood

Pretty – A Fairy Tale Retelling of the Princess Frog - *coming in November 2021*

Valor - A Fairy Tale Retelling of Jack and the Beanstalk – *Coming in December 2021*

Thank you so much for reading this book. If you want to hear more about upcoming books visit my website at KristinaJJordan.com and download your free copy of Free – the retelling of Rapunzel.

I love interacting with fantasy and fairytale readers on Facebook, Instagram, and Tiktok at my handle is @kristinajjordanauthor and I'd love to see you there.

Like all authors, I appreciate honest reviews and love hearing feedback about my books. Please feel free to leave a review on Amazon Bookbub or Goodreads.

---

1.   http://mybook.to/free

2.   http://mybook.to/bravekjj

3.   http://mybook.to/strongkjj

4.   http://mybook.to/True

Don't miss out!

Visit the website below and you can sign up to receive emails whenever Kristina J Jordan publishes a new book. There's no charge and no obligation.

https://books2read.com/r/B-A-KPEO-WWKQB

BOOKS 2 READ

Connecting independent readers to independent writers.

Also by Kristina J Jordan

The Crown and the Sceptre
Free A Fairy Tale Retelling of Rapunzel

Standalone
Brave - A Retelling of Beauty and the Beast

Made in the USA
Monee, IL
06 December 2024

72694729R00144